Night Cruiser:
Short Stories about Creepy, Amusing, or Spiritual Encounters with the Shadow

by Veronica Dale

Published by Nika Press

Nika Press

Copyright © 2014 by Veronica Dale
Nika Press
Macomb, MI 48044

ISBN 13: 978-0692344613

Many thanks to Cynthia Harrison, to Dora Badger and Woodward Press for author services, to James Price for the book cover, to Joe Ponepinto for book design and to all the talented writers at Detroit Working Writers who generously gave their suggestions and support. Without their help, and that of many others, *Night Cruiser* would never have backed out of the garage!

Praise for Night Cruiser Stories

"I read 'Persons of Marred Appearance' two or three times and discovered it was full of compact meaning. It's innovative and creative, with an author extraordinaire!"
Annick Hivert-Carthrew has written several books, including Ghostly Lights Return *and* A Pictorial History of Michigan Civilian Conservation Corps.

"'Sealing the Deal' is hysterically funny! Excellent details. I love the whole bit."
F. J. Bergmann writes speculative poetry and fiction. She is editor of the Science Fiction Poetry Association's Star*Line *journal and poetry editor of* Mobius: The Journal of Social Change. *Her many awards include the SFPA Elgin Award and the Rannu Award for Poetry.*

"'Jake and Jamal' is a thought-provoking and tragic piece, [describing] the potential of evil unleashed. Excellent."
Iris Lee Underwood's feature articles have appeared in over a dozen magazines and newspapers. She is the author of Encouraging Words for All Seasons.

"Striking and fascinating, 'Scorpio' has accomplished a lot in a short space."
Diana Dinverno is a poet and author of feature stories and essays which have appeared in Metro Detroit and national publications.

"'Night Cruiser' is a story we can all relate to! It's told in a great voice and held my interest."
Christian Belz is an architect, the author of the Ken Knoll Murder Mystery Series, *and the Grand Prize winner in Aquarius Press's Bright Harvest Prize for his short story "Chambers."*

DEAR READER...

...you might enjoy these stories at a deeper level if you know where they're coming from. A brilliant psychologist, one of my favorite authors, and a medieval mystic all inspired them.

The psychologist Carl Jung wrote about "the shadow." This is the dark side of ourselves that we don't want to look at, the thing we don't wish to be—and which therefore gets projected into our nightmares, our horror stories, and even onto other people and groups. Yet Jung believed that, if acknowledged and correctly come to terms with, "The shadow is ninety percent pure gold."

The author is J.R.R. Tolkien, who wrote about the "eucatastrophe," how a tragic event, the catastrophe, can become redemptive. His *Lord of the Rings* is a prime example of that, as are the New Testament Passion narratives.

And the mystic is a woman whose writings I discovered when I was working toward my master's degree in pastoral ministry: Julian of Norwich. In one of the most famous lines in Catholic theology, she states: "All shall be well, and all shall be well, and all manner of things shall be well."

These expressions of faith intrigued me, even though I knew they sometimes run counter to what we experience. In my work as a pastoral minister I had to face the fact that bad things can happen to good people. But I also experienced something else. I saw how men and women of every religious persuasion were able to find unexpected strength in their encounters with the dark side. They have discovered that, as Jung put it, their "considerable moral effort" in becoming conscious of the shadow also made them aware of their inner light.

The characters in these stories, as well as those in my upcoming fantasy series *Coin of Rulve*, also struggle with this encounter. They all come face-to-face with the shadow, and must decide what to do about it.

Some of these stories are disturbing, but it's the shadow's *job* to disturb. Other stories have humorous or spiritual dimensions, which have to do with *our* job: to use these uniquely human abilities to mine the shadow for its pure gold.

The first story here, "Night Cruiser," is an invitation to embark on this mining expedition. Enjoy the ride!

Contents

Night Cruiser   1

Dried Beans   4

Sealing the Deal   10

Scorpio   20

Persons of Marred Appearance   23

Within Five Feet   37

One Level Down   46

Jake and Jamal   53

Advent   58

End of Story   68

Questions for Discussion   83

NIGHT CRUISER

What's inside the dark car that prowls the street at night? A shorter version of this story was an award-winner in the Rochester Writers' Micro-Fiction Contest.

I see it from time to time, always in the middle of the night: a car moving slowly down our quiet streets. I've asked my neighbors, but no one else has ever noticed it. That's probably because my house is at the far end of our small subdivision, so I'm the only one who gets this particular perspective.

The car enters from the main road, prowls past my house, turns around at the end of the block, passes me again, and then leaves. I can't tell if it's the same car all the time, but it's not any make or model I recognize. Since we have no streetlights, I'm not sure about the color either. At night all cars are black, aren't they? But sometimes I think this one could be red.

This strikes me as odd; you'd think anyone would be able to tell the difference.

Once I was startled to see the car parked directly across the street from my house. The windows were dark, the headlights turned off. It just sat there. I watched, hidden and motionless behind the stacked vertical blinds, my heart thumping. A red point of light moved in the front seat. The lit end of a cigarette perhaps, held in an unseen hand. Was the face turned toward me? Studying me? I eased back from the window and returned to my chair in the living room. It's a comfortable chair, conformed to my shape after many years. I tried to read under the bright circle cast by the table lamp, but my mind was outside in the dark. When I looked again, the car was gone.

It's important that you know I have a life. I go to work, have lunch with friends, watch the 11 o'clock news. It's always the same: the same bodies found in wooded areas, the same home invaders, the same invisible drive-by shooters.

Before going to bed I make sure all the doors are locked, then watch the street. The few cars I see belong to neighbors. They pull into their driveway and the garage door rises. The car slides into a lighted place and the door descends. The street is left in its usual isolation.

It came again last night. I spotted it around two in the morning, just as it turned into the first block of my E-shaped subdivision. I waited. It emerged and glided into the next street. I could see it: slowly searching, its headlights passing between the houses. Within minutes, the car reappeared, coming toward me. Its headlights blazed into my eyes, but I stood completely still. Had I been seen? Perhaps as a ghost, dressed in white?

Apparently not. The car turned in front of my house and went on. It's a short block and I knew what would happen. A red sheen appeared among the trees as the tail-lights brightened. For several heart-beats I saw nothing, heard nothing, until the car emerged from the shadows and made its way back toward my house. At the curb, it paused. Someone inside was staring at me. I could feel it.

After a while, the car moved on. I knew it would come back. One night it would pull into my driveway, turn off its lights, and wait.

What would I do? How could I go to bed, knowing it was out there?

I could leave the house and step into the night. I could approach the driver's side window. I could bend and peer inside. Would I see only my face in the mirror-blackness, or would I see something else as the glass slowly descended?

DRIED BEANS

A tortured spirit has haunted three generations of women, and now it challenges a little girl. This story won First Prize in the Julia Grice Fiction Contest and was published in the St. Anthony Messenger Magazine.

A sharp rattle awoke her. Heart pounding, Lottie turned to look at the pitch-black rectangle of the open bedroom door. From down the hall it came again, the sound she dreaded, of dried beans flung like pebbles across the linoleum floor. A chill skittered down her arms.

She waited, holding her breath, but the sound was not repeated. The feel of a ghostly presence slowly ebbed away. She must clean up the mess before her husband saw it in the morning. He worked the early shift at Dodge Main, on the assembly line where the new 1949 Coronets were coming through.

Quietly, so as not to wake Martin, she slid to the edge of the bed. The springs creaked and he grabbed her arm so roughly that she took a sharp breath. "What you get up for?" he demanded. "Lay down."

He'd spent some time at the beer garden again, so she knew enough to obey. Had the ghost disturbed little Anna? No sound came from her daughter's cot at the foot of their bed. Lottie waited until Martin's breathing roughened into snores, and then summoned the courage to slip down the hall to the kitchen. The light from the bare bulb revealed that navy beans had been strewn over the floor again. The glass jar had been taken from the pantry and sat empty in the middle of the oilcloth-covered kitchen table.

The ghost lady had done it. Wanda Malaski next door said the wife of the previous renter had hung herself in the pantry. Now her ghost emerged from time to time, voiceless and restless, to fling hard beans on the floor. Glancing over her shoulder at the unlit opening to the pantry, Lottie scooped up the beans and poured them back in the jar.

After novena last Friday, she had told Fr. Wujek about the ghost, and he said to pray for the woman's soul. While she was talking to him, Lottie hoped he wouldn't notice her swollen eye. If Father had asked about it, she would have said she bumped into a door.

"What's the matter, Mama?"

Lottie whirled to see Anna standing there, nervously rubbing the sleeve of her flannel nightgown between her thumb and forefinger.

"*Nic*, sweetheart. Go back to bed."

Behind the child, Martin loomed out of the dark. "What's all this noise? Can't a working man get sleep in his own house?" He pushed Anna roughly toward their bedroom.

Lottie backed away, but Martin hit her anyway. She tasted blood inside her cheek and swallowed it.

Anna grew up, her mom and dad passed away, and now she too was married. It was 1969. With her baby daughter in her arms, Anna shifted her sore back against the rocking chair and stared at the brightly-colored globs oozing up and down in the lava lamp. Turning away from her almost empty bottle, little Kimberly watched them too, until her eyes glazed and finally closed. Anna tucked the child into her crib and shut the door. Her husband's voice emerged from their bedroom down the hall. "Get in here, for godsake. I gotta get up at four in the morning."

Anna obeyed and slid into bed beside him. Their love-making was over quickly and tasted of cheap whiskey. He fell asleep and Anna lay quiet, not daring to toss or turn. Her mind wandered to a ghost story her mother used to tell, about the soul of a troubled woman who threw dried beans on the floor.

Why dried beans? Odd she had never asked herself that question before. Perhaps the beans were all the thin, ghostly hands could lift. Perhaps the poor soul was desperate to be heard, to be acknowledged, but didn't have the strength to shatter cups or break dishes.

Her mother said she prayed for the woman's soul and the ghost went away. Anna used to pray—for a happy family life, for a husband who didn't drink—but her prayers never worked. Her secret sorrow never went away. She hoped life would be different for her daughter.

That night she dreamed of things that rattled: a baby toy, chains, dried beans scattered like seeds on a hard kitchen floor.

Anna's daughter Kimberly grew up and decided she wouldn't live the kind of life her mother had. She was a woman of the '90's and could choose not to get married at all. In the next fifteen years she'd had a succession of boyfriends, the latest being Shawn. He came around when he felt like it and sometimes paid for part of the rent. The greatest love in Kimberly's life was her daughter Emma. Emma's father was one of the boyfriends, who had left abruptly before she was born.

Seven-year-old Emma sat quietly at a table with her second-grade class. She felt like crying, because Shawn hit Mommy again last night. She wanted to scream at him—"stop! stop!"—but was afraid he'd hit her again, too. She sneaked a look at her teacher, Miss Kathy. Miss Kathy always looked so worried whenever she asked about a bruise on her arm or cheek. "If an adult is hitting you," Miss Kathy told the class, "you have to tell. Even if it's your mom or your mom's boyfriend or your step-dad."

But Emma never told. Mommy said not to.

Miss Kathy walked around the table and Emma ducked her head. She didn't want her teacher to see the mark on her chin, where Shawn had pinched her so hard he made her cry. And made her angry, too. She didn't do anything wrong and it just wasn't fair.

Her teacher stopped, then crouched down beside her. "What's this?" Gently she touched the spot.

"Nothing. I fell on some steps."

"Are you sure?"

Emma nodded, biting her lip.

Her teacher sighed, got up, and spoke to the class. "Tomorrow we're going to learn how to grow a plant. Then you can give the plant to your mothers for Mother's Day. Does anyone have seeds at home they can bring to school?"

Emma raised her hand. "I can bring dried navy beans," she said proudly. "My mom has them around in case she wants to make the kind of soup my great-grandma used to make."

One of the students spoke up. "Those kind of beans won't work. They're too dry to sprout."

"Maybe not," Miss Kathy said. "You never know about the power of a seed. Bring them, Emma, and we'll see what happens."

The next morning, Mommy and Shawn argued again and Shawn shoved her against the refrigerator. After he went to work, Mommy grabbed the plastic bag of dried navy beans from the kitchen counter and threw it very hard on the floor. The bag broke and beans scattered everywhere. She was crying as the two of them picked up the beans and put some of them into a plastic container for school. "This can't go on," Mommy sobbed. "It just can't."

Emma didn't know what to say, but after her mom stopped crying, she told Emma the story about her great-grandmother and the ghost who threw dried beans.

"Why did the ghost lady do that?" Emma asked.

Mom was filling a pot with water and didn't look at her. "Maybe she was married to someone like Shawn," she muttered.

At school, Miss Kathy smiled as she took the container full of beans. Following the teacher's directions, Emma filled a styrofoam cup with dirt from a big bag that had "potting soil" written on it, poked a navy bean into it, and then carefully poured a little water over the seed.

I hate Shawn, she thought, *and never want to see Mommy throw beans on the floor again. I'm sure Miss Kathy wouldn't either.* Emma put her cup on the windowsill, where the sun would shine on it, and glanced over her shoulder at her teacher.

Maybe she should tell.

No, it would be better to wait and see what the seed would do.

Every school day she made sure to water it. Then, on Saturday night, the sound of Mommy and Shawn arguing again woke her up. She was too afraid to get out of her bed, but the next morning Mommy's jaw looked all black and blue.

"She slipped and fell on the kitchen floor," Shawn said. He looked at her with those little pig eyes and smiled, as if he dared her to say anything different.

On Monday morning at school, Emma ran to the windowsill. A little green stem, with its head still in the dirt, had appeared. In only a short time it stood up straight and sprouted two fat leaves.

"See, boys and girls?" Miss Kathy said. "That dried bean looked dead on the outside, but look what was inside it all this time."

Dried beans were amazing. And they were brave, too, reaching out with their leafy arms. Emma made up her mind. You should cook dried beans or plant them, but never have to throw them on the floor. As the children filed out for recess, she approached her teacher's desk.

SEALING THE DEAL

A young woman has to bargain for her life with a confused, time-traveling sorcerer. Among the most submissions ever received by Penumbra Magazine, this story was a finalist for their Superheroes issue.

I had no sense of foreboding whatsoever when I changed into my flannel PJs—no Victoria's Secret nightgown for me: too lacy and itchy—and looked out the window before going to bed. Maybe I'd spot a raccoon or—What was *that?* A perpendicular strip of light, which definitely hadn't been there seconds ago, glowed several feet away in the dark.

The strip rapidly expanded into an open doorway, which hovered in the air. I barely had time to blink in disbelief when a dark shape rushed out, the doorway disappeared, and someone zoomed right through the window and into my room.

"Agh!" I cried, whirling.

"Ah *ha!*" the creature yelled. "I have you now, Lorndred." It pointed a wooden staff at me and its tip glowed ominously.

"Don't shoot!" I put my hands up. "I'm not Lorndred!"

"Eh?" An old man about four feet high and wearing a dirt-colored robe peered at me through a tangled mess of grey hair and beard. "You are not the Dark

Lord." He looked around, as if seeing my bedroom for the first time. "This is not Por Drak." His eyes turned back to me and ran down my flannel-clad body. "You are not even a man."

"What—who are you?" The staff was still pointed at me and it still glowed.

A look of cunning crossed his face. "Oh, no. I trust no innocent looks. Just call me Mothball."

At least that's what I thought he said. "Mothball?"

"Your accent is terrible. It is *Mueth*-bal. You must wrinkle the nose when you say it."

I glanced at the staff and wrinkled my nose. "*Moth-ball*," I said. "Now please, stop pointing that—that thing at me."

Apparently deciding I wasn't dangerous, he lowered his staff. The glow winked out.

"Why are you shaking?" he demanded. "Have you some disease?"

"You scared me! Who the hell are you? How the hell did you get here?" Normally I don't swear, but the words just came out.

He pulled himself up to his full height. "I come not from hell!" His eyes shifted warily about. "This is not hell, is it?"

"What? This is Michigan. Actually, we do have a Hell here, but it's a small town, more of a tourist attraction." Taking a tentative step toward him, I held out my right palm—to show him the map of our state—and pointed to where Hell was. "See, it's here. Not too far from Pinckney."

He peered into my palm. "I do not see any towns."

"Of course not! It's like a map. This area where you, uh, landed is shaped like a mitten."

"Ah." He cleared his throat. "I seem to have come

to the wrong place. A slight error. Too much atherain again. Or maybe not enough."

"You should go home," I said fervently. "You're making me very nervous. Where is home, anyway?"

"None of your business," he said. Then something seemed to occur to him and he frowned. "Who taught you to speak Paracor?"

"What? I'm speaking English."

"Sqiglish? Gibberish? You certainly are."

I didn't know what to make of this, so said nothing. Apparently his magic powers, or whatever, enabled him to hear me in his language and vice versa. A hundred questions wanted to tumble out of my mouth, but they all got stuck in the door, like the Three Stooges.

"I will go home," he said, "but you must give me something first. To pay for my expenses, you know. They are considerable."

"Why should *I* pay? *You're* the one who made a mistake."

He raised his staff and glowered at me.

"Well, maybe we could arrange something," I said.

"Fetch a lantern. I want to look around."

I flicked the switch and light flooded the room.

"Agh!" Mothball flung his hand over his eyes, jerked back, and knocked over the floor lamp. He waved his staff wildly and I dived to the floor just in time. A fire-bolt cracked over my head and seared a gash in the ceiling.

"Stop it!" I yelled. "It's just a light. No one's trying to hurt you." I peeped around the bed at him.

He lowered his staff and looked around. "How did you do that?"

I showed him the light switch. He cautiously flicked it off and on; then, grinning like a child with a new toy, several times in rapid succession. At last he gestured toward the overhead light.

"I will take that home with me."

"Uh, it won't work there. You need electricity, which I gather you don't have."

"What is this *elektree*? Explain yourself."

I tried, but I don't know much about voltage and power plants, and I could see I was just making him angry. Which I definitely didn't want to do. I remembered an item stashed in the back of my closet. "Allow me," I said in my most enticing voice, "to give you something else."

He raised his bushy eyebrows. "Such as?"

With my hands patting the air to keep him calm, I ducked inside and quickly emerged with a picture my mom bought at a garage sale. Somehow it wound up with my stuff when I moved out. "See? It's Elvis, painted on real velvet. Feel how soft—."

"That is definitely not elvish. They have a very different style." He brandished his staff. "I warn you, wench. Do not try to cheat me."

"No, no. You misunderstand. This is a picture of a man called El-vis." I pronounced the name carefully. "He was very famous. Rich, too. They called him the King of Rock and—."

"No kings. I have had bad experiences with kings. And with rocks as well, if you must know."

"Oh. I'm sorry."

His interest suddenly seemed to be caught by my hair, which he studied with narrowed eyes. "Why were you shorn? For what criminal act?"

"Shorn?"

He reached out and grabbed a handful of hair. "They obviously cut your locks for a reason."

"Stop that!" I said, pushing his hand away. "I'm not a criminal. I'm a law-abiding citizen. I work at"—I was about to blurt out "Burger King," but remembered his previous remark just in time—"a respectable wayside inn."

"So you are a sinner, then. Shorn for your sins."

I opened my mouth, but what could I say? There was too wide a gap between us. I shut it again.

"Perhaps," he mused, "I should take you. Young wenches are always in demand. Especially sinful ones."

I must have squeaked.

"But no," he went on. "Too skinny and pale. No good for the fields—or the bed either, by the look of you. What about your mate? Is he big and strong?"

I thought of my boyfriend Devon, still a student at the local community college. He wore glasses, loved Dungeons and Dragons, and probably weighed around 130 pounds. "Yes he is," I stated. "And he'll be home from—from the mines—any minute now. He won't like you being here at all."

"Mines? You have silstrum? Ciela crystals?" A greedy light appeared in his eyes. "Show me these mines."

"They're just coal mines," I said, thinking quickly. "Full of dirty, messy coal that you wouldn't be interested in at all. But I have in my possession something you would be interested in." I dashed to my jewelry box, which I bought on sale from K Mart, and pulled out a handful of green and purple beads I got years ago from a Mardi Gras party. "Take all these jewels, these bright and glittering jewels, and go away."

He barely glanced at them. "Baubles. My apprentice wears better. What else do you have?"

"A mate. A jealous mate, on his way home right now."

"So you said." Mothball smiled in a way I didn't like. He sat down on the only upholstered chair in the room, the olive green one from my parents' basement. "We will wait for him then. A big, strong slave will bring me about thirty ducats."

Uh oh, I thought. *Now what? Should I call 911? No, I'd just get in trouble for making what they'd think was a crank call.*

"I couldn't afford to keep him myself," Mothball mused. "Food is so costly." He sighed.

"You really don't want to wait for my mate," I said. "He could actually, uh, bite your head off."

"Sounds like Lorndred," he said gloomily. "The dark lord of Por Drak. He wields—."

"Yes," I said hastily. Devon went on and on about who wielded what in his role-playing games. "I've heard of people like him."

"Then you understand why I must confront him and save the Sooths."

"I certainly do. So let's—let's get you back home so you can confront him as soon as possible. We'll look around for something to pay your expenses and then you can leave right away. Far less risky than waiting for someone who could bite your head off."

"Perhaps you are right." He climbed to his feet. "But I must leave before first light, and if I find nothing of value to bring back, it will have to be you." He tapped a front tooth, thinking. "The Mecthlid might take you. As an appetizer perhaps."

I didn't ask who or what Mecthlid was. I didn't want to know.

We began the search. I thought it would be ridiculously easy. This was the twenty-first century after all, and full of modern marvels. I should be able to find a dozen things Mothball would be eager to take back.

I led him to the medicine cabinet in the bathroom. "Ibuprofen!" I cried, snatching the bottle out. "It relieves pain in a jiffy."

I poured a few tablets into my hand and held them out to Mothball. He looked at them dubiously. "Chalk, looks like. Most unimpressive." Suspicion crept into his eyes. "Could even be poison, could it not?"

"No! I'll prove it to you." I turned the water on and reached for the plastic cup, intending to swallow a pill myself.

Mothball gasped and stared. "This!" he shouted. "I will take this!" He pulled at the sink with both hands.

I managed to wrench him away from it before he broke something; plumbers around here charge $80 just to walk through the door. "You can't! It's connected to all kinds of pipes. To pipes inside the walls." This, too, took a lot of explaining on my part, but at last he seemed to understand.

"What is this elixir?" Mothball jabbed a knobby finger at the bottle of bright red mouthwash.

"It's for bad breath."

"Bad Breath." He seized the bottle. "To accompany the Evil Eye!"

"No!" Mouthwash too took some explanation, but at last we plunged on, into my small living room.

"A black box," he muttered with raised eyebrows, eyeing the TV.

Without thinking, I turned it on. His shriek scared the wits out of me. I finally got him settled down on the couch, but it took a while before I could drag him away from Conan the Barbarian. He wanted the TV, of course, but there was that electricity thing again. No sense even mentioning my cell phone.

We moved into the kitchen. He thought the refrigerator was a door to somewhere, but eventually wound up eating the last slice of pizza. He poked his long nose into the shelves of canned goods, none of which he believed was actual food. He liked the Frosted Flakes, but deemed one box wasn't enough to seal our bargain. By now the sky outside was turning grey and I was getting frantic. He followed me as I rushed from room to room.

"A vase of silk roses that will never wilt?"

He attempted to smell them, but the dust made him sneeze.

"My watch?"

Who wanted a glassy eye that watched him all the time?

"I'm sure these cool Nikes would fit you."

They were obviously torture devices and he wouldn't even try them on.

"Look, a flashlight!"

The batteries didn't work.

We wound up back in the kitchen. Mothball glanced out the window, then turned glumly toward me. "First light. Your world has nothing to offer." He raised his staff and reached for me. "We must go."

"Wait!" I said, backing away. "I just thought of something. Your potions. Your herbs and things. How do you store them?

"In jars. In phials and pouches and decanters. Why?"

"Do they get dried out? Spill? Lose their power after a while?"

"Naturally. There is no way to prevent that."

"But there is!" I said triumphantly. I opened the

bottom kitchen cabinet and a bunch of plastic containers fell out. My sister used to be a Tupperware lady and these were mostly birthday and Christmas presents from her. They seemed to have accumulated over the years.

"Look at this!" I seized one of the square containers—Freezer-Mates, I think they're called—and filled it with water. I sealed the cover and shook it. I dropped it on the floor. "See? Nothing spills. Great for traveling." I grabbed a good-sized Modular Mate and filled it with Frosted Flakes. "These will stay nice and crispy for weeks. Your herbs will stay fresh for much longer." I fished out my big Thatsa Bowl. "Think how good this would be for—for heads and entrails and things. No leakage. No smells."

"Hmm," he said, bending to look into the cabinet. "These would stack nicely on my work table. I see they come in bright colors and all kinds of sizes. They are transparent; yet do not break like glass."

"Here, you can have all these." I stuffed as many containers as I could into the Thatsa Bowl and thrust it into his hands.

He squinted at them. "They don't need wires or pipes in the walls?"

"No. Nice and simple for every world. And if you aren't completely satisfied, just bring them back." *If you can find your way*, I thought deviously.

He hesitated, looked at the bowl, looked at me, then out the window. It was dawn. He raised his staff.

I winced.

With a flash of light he was gone. Just like that. I was alone in my kitchenette.

Wow.

Using only my wits, I had defeated a powerful wizard. Devon would admire that no end. With a smile and a swagger, I headed back to bed.

If one of that ilk should appear again, I'd handle the situation just fine: buy him off with duct tape and a few zip-lock bags.

SCORPIO

The creepiest shadow is always the one you project onto others.

Have you seen that awful news story, about a one-year-old with her family on vacation in Belize? The child was screaming and no one knew why. It turned out her daddy had unknowingly put her shoe on that morning with a scorpion inside. A shame he wasn't more observant.

There's a constellation called Scorpio, you know. Up north where I grew up, it crouches low among the trees and houses. But here in the New Mexican desert, you can clearly see it above the horizon: the baleful red eye of its main star, the claws, the vicious, curved tail.

In astrology, Scorpio is a swampy water sign. People born under this sign notice everything, forget nothing, and hold grudges. They are noted for their piercing green eyes, for relationships with the dead.

The grandmother I'm named after was a Scorpio. She took me in after my mother died. My grandmother had a secret mean streak. Just to scare me, she said she could speak to dead people. I don't remember much about her, except for the strong grip of her bony hands and her crooked yellow teeth. She drank too much and her bedroom didn't have a closet, only a heavy oak wardrobe that locked from the outside. If you got stuck in there, too bad. No matter how you screamed and pounded on that door, it wouldn't budge. I guess my grandmother discovered this for herself, because that's where they discovered her body.

I never had children, only two miscarriages. Both would have been Scorpios. Once I realized this, I found that the feel of those little clawed creatures growing inside me was quite unpleasant. When they died, I felt relieved. It was for the best.

Scorpions lurk in unexpected places: in the creases of your easy chair, in the folds of the blanket you bought in a bazaar, even—and this really happened to someone I know—in a Monopoly game box. Ordinary, even comforting places where you don't expect the sting of a poisonous tail. I once picked up a book I'd been reading—it was called *People of the Lie*—and opened it to the bookmark. And there it was. Black and hairy and ready to spring. I screamed and threw the book across the room, but never found the creature. It had completely disappeared.

The book was about what the author, a psychologist, called the "evil personality disorder." I could see that every one of his case studies involved a Scorpio. The book wound up in the garbage, though. I couldn't take a chance on opening it again.

My mother was a Scorpio, born in late October. She drowned; suicide they said. I'm not surprised she couldn't live with herself. Mother was the kind of person who held her venom in reserve, let it fester, then whipped the barb into your skin. My ex-husband was like her—vindictive and caustic. Poisonous people both, and frankly, I'm glad they're gone.

Did I mention a new family has moved in next

door? They have a little boy who would have been the same age as one of mine. He is blond and cheerful—a Gemini, I thought at first. It came as quite a shock when I learned his birthday is on Halloween.

Not good. Not good at all. I must make sure to baby-sit him sometime, and make things right.

PERSONS OF MARRED APPEARANCE

A once state-of-the-art android exerts an unusual influence on the woman who ruined him and the grieving deacon who is now responsible for him. This story won an honorable mention out of 18,000 submissions in a Writer's Digest Genre Short Story Contest and was a semi-finalist for the William Van Dyke Short Story Contest.

A soft ping woke her. Her husband's face filled the entire wall-screen, his ice-blue eyes looking over her head and his lips frozen in a smile. Deirdre activated the message. "I bought you some company for when I'm gone," Bernard said. "An FF10 Real-eyz. The price tag put me back a few bucks; but, hey babe, you deserve it. Happy anniversary." The message blanked off and Deirdre's face stared back at her from the mirrored wall.

Bernard would not be alone at the conference tonight. Another woman would be all over him. But he made damn sure the wife got what she deserved.

She made herself a Bloody Mary for breakfast and found the latest model of FF10 technology waiting in the front hall. It was gazing at El Salvador, the full-size crucifix that hung in the foyer. Given the abhorrence of human suffering programmed into its kind, the fact that it could look at the carving at all was unusual. None of the household droids would come near it.

"So what do you think?" Deirdre asked, leaning against the wall.

The construct turned its liquid brown eyes to her. Just as the ads proclaimed, its finely honed face hinted at strength and sensitivity, and its bronze silicone gel-skin suggested the heritage of many races. "A graphic depiction," it said, "of the divine experiencing human anguish."

"Actually, it's an original Lopez-Guerra."

"Yes, I can see that. The style is unique."

"My husband acquired it from the local monastery, and thereby saved its financial bacon." She held up her glass in a mock toast: "To the most valuable piece of art in the house."

The construct ducked its head and smiled. "Actually, that would be me."

"Oh, I'm sure it is." When Bernard wanted to make a point, he spared no expense.

Rolling an ice cube in her mouth, she showed it through the rooms and pointed out the artifacts Bernard acquired when he bought what was left of the national park: Puebloan pots, Anasazi blankets, slabs of petroglyphs removed from rock-faces. She waved her hand at a pickax mounted above their king-size bed.

"This lovely item dates back to Mormon pioneer days. The owner inscribed his name and date on the handle, so it's worth big money to collectors."

"An odd place to hang it," the FF remarked.

She snorted. "The symbolism amuses Bernard."

Troubled lines appeared between the construct's

eyebrows, but it didn't say anything. She downed the last of her drink. "So, FF10, what's your name?"

"At default—level five—I'm Chris. Pleased to meet you." It held out a hand.

She grinned and thrust her empty glass into it. "Make me another one of these, Chris."

That afternoon she went golfing. The watered greens contrasted vividly with the red sands of the Utah desert, and she caught glimpses of herself, distorted and brightly painted, in the wraparound sunglasses of her friends. They flirted with the caddies, then had dinner at the clubhouse: chicken Caesar salads and lots of Shiraz.

"I got me the new Fully Functional," Deirdre announced.

"An FF10? We've got to see it!"

Back at the house, they arranged themselves on the long sofas, and Deirdre ordered a pitcher of sangrias from their Household 34. She summoned Chris.

"Tell us what you can do, Chris."

Its Real-eyz shone. "Quite a lot, actually. I can give comfort in all kinds of ways, like chakra massage, reiki, and pheromone therapy. I can play music from many times and places. I'm pretty well versed in a variety of topics—like art, religion, and science—but I learn from speaking with you." The FF smiled, and the glow in its eyes increased. "It's a pleasure to learn."

"The hell with that kind of pleasure." Valerie giggled and turned to Deirdre. "Let's get to the Full Fun part."

"Disrobe, Chris," Deirdre commanded.

It did so, then spread out its arms. "So who do you want, ladies?" it asked. "Crystal at four and below, or Christopher at six and up?"

"Go up!"

It looked at Deirdre.

"Eight," she ordered.

The FF seemed to take a breath. The chest expanded, shoulders muscled, a male member appeared.

"Hell-o Christopher," Deirdre said.

"Oh, my God!" the women exclaimed, their eyes sparkling with alcohol. "What a hunk!"

They played for a while and Deirdre went up to nine, but she wouldn't go ten. "That's just for me," she said.

After her friends left, she sank into her overstuffed chair and sipped a vodka martini.

He—at level nine she couldn't help but think of it as a he—remained standing in the middle of the room.

"So much alcohol isn't good for you," he said.

"You sound just like Bernard." She was slurring her words but didn't care.

"Deirdre, it's been hours and I need to default. Let's relax. I'll rustle up a snack for us and then play some of my favorite music. It's neo-medieval and I think you'd like it."

It was night, and the tall black windows reflected the only human being in the house, talking to a machine. "Shut up," she ordered. "Go ten." It was what she deserved, wasn't it?

She took him to bed and worked hard for release, but nothing came. She clawed at his warm gel-skin, as if it were a barrier. "Get rough with me, Christopher. Godammit, batter my heart!"

He ran his strong hand down her arm. "I can't hurt you, Deirdre. I can but breathe, shine, and seek to mend."

She stiffened. "What are you talking about?"

The dark eyes looked at her. "I'm quoting from a poem. Weren't you?"

"I don't want stupid poetry! I want everything you've got!"

"It's a poem about love."

Behind him, the walls were spinning. Like big mirrors, they swept past. They reflected the smeared lipstick on her face, the pale larva of her middle-aged body, the hands like claws that clutched a tin man. A full-size image swung into view, and it was that of Bernard's frozen sneer.

"What do you know about love?" she shouted. "You're nothing but a goddamn sex-bot!" She slid out of bed and the floor tilted under her bare feet. Stumbling, she grabbed the pickax off its hooks and turned to the face in the mirror. The pickax felt awkward and heavy as she raised it.

"Please put that down," Christopher said. "You'll hurt yourself."

"Go to hell, Christopher. Just go to hell!"

He jumped in front of her as she swung, and the ax hit him in the face. With a sharp exhale, he staggered backward. Defaulting, he slid onto the floor.

Oh God, what had she done? She moaned, but the huge face above her continued to smirk. *"Can't even get that right, can you, babe?"*

She wrenched the ax free and, with a grunt and a satisfying heave, shattered the big mirror and everything in it.

The household droids stood silently at the door as Bernard regarded the wreckage of the FF and his wife. The former lay motionless, its face split open. The latter sat shivering in a corner of the room, shards from the wall-mirror glinting in her hair. Bernard picked up the ax and cradled it in his arms; but its inscription had been scratched and it was worthless to him now.

He turned to his assistant. "Get this FF out of here. Patch it up, send it through reprogramming, then donate it somewhere as a tax write-off. And for god-sake, get her shrink to make a house call!"

It was a third-rate repair job: the repro stood before him, its face seamed and askew. How fitting they assigned orientation to me, lay deacon William thought. Let the dead bury the dead. "Tell me your name."

It blinked, accessing and processing, as if it were decades ago. "Christmas," it said in a toneless voice. "Chrysalis. Crystal."

It had once been the newest technology on the planet, and now it didn't even know its own name. "Your documentation says Chris."

Blink, blink. "Correct."

"What can you do, Chris?" Repros usually couldn't do much.

"I am suited for menial service. I learn from conversing with you. Crystals are alive. They have structure and grow."

While it was being repaired, William wondered, had it been self-aware but unable to communicate? The thought brought too many bad memories and he pushed it away. "Follow me, Chris. We have several other droids in the monastery, and you will take orders from Dolores, our H28."

They took the short-cut through the baptistry, its skylight grey in the twilight, and skirted the edge of the dark, still pool. Chris stopped in front of the bank of flickering votive candles. "Did you light these?"

"I don't light candles." Katia used to. On certain quiet evenings before they went to bed.

The repro pointed at the life-sized crucifix hanging above the votives. "Emmanuel," it stated. "Translation: God-with-us."

God hadn't been anywhere around the last two years: not in the doctors' offices, not at the hospital, not at the funeral or during his months at Havencrest. "Emmanuel's a Christmas word," William said, "and Christmas is for kids. This is El Salvador, a reproduction of a famous original that used to be displayed here."

The FF turned to gaze at him with its blank metal eyes. "A grappling implication of the divine," it said, "dispersed in human anguish."

"Ignore it, Chris. It happened a long time ago, and there's nothing you could have done."

Chris was not very useful, but the monks agreed it was certainly the ideal of poverty, chastity, and obedience. The abbot ordered it be kept away from the paying customers who came to the monastery for retreats. Some of them would be shocked to find a former Full Fun on church property and others would be put off by its ruined face. So Chris worked mostly at night—cleaning the bathrooms, watering the plants, mopping the quiet marble halls.

After several weeks, the repro came into William's office. "May I converse with the people who visit here? I can relieve pain and give comfort in kindly ways, including chalky massage, ray keys, and feeble therapy. I am a verse of neo-music from many times and—."

"That's just an old program talking. You're no longer what you once were."

Chris touched its face. "I am a person of marred appearance. Isaiah 52:14. Perhaps I frighten others."

"Not if you stay out of sight."

Chris looked up at the stained-glass window behind the desk. "That is Jesus by the seashore. He is the fishing man."

William turned back to his work. "That window hasn't been washed in a long time, Chris. Try and get to it tomorrow."

That evening William found that Chris had wandered into the baptistry, where it might startle one of the guests. It stood at the top of the shallow steps, gazing into the pool. "What are you doing here, Chris?"

It didn't look up. "I am watching the water. It is burning."

"No. Those are only reflections of the votive-lights."

"A fish is down there."

"It's not real, Chris. It's a religious symbol, part of a mosaic."

Still not looking at him, it took a step forward.

"Stop. You can't go into the pool."

It blinked several times, trying to access what must be a tumbling, fragmented data stream. "In a chrysalis," it said, "the larva dissolves down to the molecular level, and then is re-formed."

"So you want to be the first-born of the dead?"

The repro turned its head toward him. "I do not understand."

"It's your programming. Call it your humility. It won't let you see that most human beings aren't really alive. You are envying the dead."

"In baptism one drowns, shines, and seeks to mend."

"No. Total immersion will only destroy you." Perhaps that's what it wanted. It was, after all, intelligent.

"In the water one is ignited, and goes from solo to united."

"None of that pertains to you, Chris. You have no soul."

The repro extended an open hand. "But I have gone to hell. Therefore I must have a soul."

William noted the seamed plaskin that looked like scars, the blank metal eyes. It had no sex anymore and the logical mind was damaged beyond repair. A sudden, unreasoning compassion flooded him. Ironic it was only for a ruined construct, and not for the human beings he was supposed to be ministering to.

It rained the next morning. The abbot entered William's narrow office while Chris was washing the stained-glass window there. "I need you to conduct the communion service at Havencrest this afternoon," the abbot said. He placed a round pyx container, big enough to hold twenty wafers, on the desk.

William shifted in his chair. "It's too soon."

"You've got hours to prepare, and it's only next door."

"You know what I mean. I'm the last one who should do it."

"You are the last one. Marco has the flu, Elena's out of town, and Chan Li's conducting a retreat."

"Most of the patients won't even know I'm there."

"You don't have to be relevant, William, only faithful." The abbot pushed the pyx closer to him and left the room.

Chris shuffled forward. "If you are reluctant, Deacon William, let me conduct the service."

A machine might as well, William thought, given the faith I'd bring to it. "The church wouldn't approve."

"But I am named for a saint, the patron of travelers. The Christ-bearer, who carried the holy child across a stormy river."

"No you aren't. Christopher was removed from the official list of saints a long time ago. There's no proof he ever existed."

The slow mind processed, and William turned his attention back to his laptop. Why, he wondered, had he denied it this small grace?

Chris interrupted him, pointing to rain running down the glass. "Look, William. I am crying. It is the rain of God."

That not-yet time, William thought, when every tear will be wiped away. He stared at the spreadsheet in front of him, at the vast number of blank boxes that flowed beyond the screen and into the netherworld, like empty calendar squares in a long line of days.

That afternoon he followed the abbot's orders and did his job as a deacon. He filled the pyx with communion hosts and went to Havencrest. About ten people waited for him. They sat on folding chairs which faced a cloth-covered card table in a corner of the community room.

"Father," a young man inquired anxiously, "what if Jesus was born dead? Would it still count? What if he came as a man with two minds?"

The woman next to him frowned. "Watch your mouth. God'll get you. God always gets to you."

I'm bringing nothing to them, William thought. No faith, no solutions, no real presence. He said the prayers, dispersed the hosts. "The body of Christ," he said to those who came forward. "The body of Christ."

After the service William watched them go: burdened Christophers every one, wading through their stormy lives.

He took the short-cut back to his office, through the baptistry. The brief rain had passed, and under the skylight the pool sparkled with sun. Four household droids stood at the edge looking down, and he followed their collective gaze.

Under shifting, dazzling water-stars, Chris lay motionless on the bottom, his arms out, his metal eyes reflecting the light.

At mid-afternoon William watched a recycling company take the android away. They should leave it here, he told himself, for our meditation—Chris Emmanuel, lost with us. Our undead creation, destroyed in a search for what we supposedly possess. He took a deep sigh. Chris had achieved a kind of resurrection after all: his components would become part of devices like e-readers and smart phones that people used every day.

Unable to sleep that night, William rose and passed through the baptistry. An unlit votive light stood at the rim of the pool. Almost hidden in the shadows, the droids stood silently against the paneled wall, like dark carvings of disciples. They looked at the votive, then at him.

"I don't light candles," he said.

The next morning, a visitor named Deirdre Lawler entered William's office. "They told me you're the one I should see," she said. "About six months ago, my ex-husband donated an android here. An FF10 repro."

He motioned her onto to a seat opposite his desk. As she placed her handbag on the floor, he realized that she and her husband were the couple who had purchased the original El Salvador. Their photo hung in the front lobby. But she looked very different now—no make-up, no perfect smile, nothing covering the few streaks of gray.

"The android isn't here. It had to be recycled."

"Oh."

"I'm sorry." It took courage, he knew, for a woman like her not to wear make-up. Courage, or a kind of acquiescence. Katia didn't wear it after the last diagnosis.

"Actually, my counselor thought coming here might help," Deirdre said. "You see, Chris was why I finally wound up at Havencrest." She cleared her throat. "In any case, I'm sober now and mean to keep it like that. I thought I'd tie up loose ends, make sure Chris worked out all right. Since I was the one who wrecked it."

"It's the human condition," he said. "Things around us get wrecked."

She made a small gesture with her hand. "The FF wasn't really alive, so I couldn't have killed it. It was me who died—a part of me, anyway. Our marriage was dying too, and I just—finished it off."

"How long were you married?"

She smiled faintly. "To be frank, I don't think we ever were. We had a wedding, but Bernard had other women and I had my booze. Marriage doesn't work in that kind of foursome."

He understood. Cancer had been an unwelcome third party in his and Katia's relationship.

Deirdre had been honest with him, and he felt the need to respond in kind. "I spent time in Havencrest. About a year ago." There weren't many people to whom he'd admitted that.

She said nothing, only nodded.

The sun cast reflections from the stained glass window onto the desk between them. Its golden fish seemed to hover beneath the pond-dark wood. Odd how he'd never noticed that. How long, he wondered, had he been seeing things as if they had no depth?

"I was at your communion service the other day," she said. "I don't think you saw me."

"It wasn't much of a service."

"We weren't much of a congregation. But it was good of you to come. I was raised a Catholic, and it meant a lot to me." Her eyes turned liquid, but she swallowed and picked up her handbag. "Well, I've taken up enough of your time."

"Will you be all right?" Blurted out, the question dismayed him. Others had asked it of him at the funeral, and the words had seemed thoughtless and cruel. Until this moment he hadn't realized that they arose from an awkward desire to comfort.

She gave him a grateful glance. "I'll be fine. I found a small place north of town. Quiet, where I can pick up the pieces."

They said good-bye. He had pieces to pick up too.

That night, William came upon the household droids standing in the darkened baptistry. The bank of votive candles flickered behind them and the water glimmered faintly at their feet. The unlit votive still rested at the edge of the pool.

One of the droids—it was Dolores—lifted her head and gazed at him, her eyes mute mirrors that asked for nothing. William lit a taper and, kneeling down, touched it to the votive's wick. It bloomed: a candle for the stillborn, a light for any born again. Did it shine for Katia or for himself; for the Havencrest inmates or for Deirdre who escaped? It didn't matter. The flame's sole red light darted through the water and dispersed into a myriad of glittering iterations.

The next day he packed up his few belongings and said good-bye to the monks. It was time to find a place, find a day job, and resume his ministry in the evenings. After the dimness of the monastery, the sun at first hurt his eyes. He headed north, up Mesa Drive, where the new complex was looking for a live-in caretaker. They offered a small apartment, with a view of the desert.

WITHIN FIVE FEET

Brent is convinced his wife is weaving a deadly web around him—literally. His psychologist friend has the perfect solution.

"Oh god, Vern, it's going to happen tonight." Brent stared at his neighbor, his heart racing with terror. "She's going to eat me tonight."

Perched on the leather hassock, the counselor smiled slightly. "Is that so bad?"

"Are you insane? Of course that's bad!"

"Look at it this way. You go in the prime of life. You avoid the nursing home, the wheelchair, and the fear of getting squashed in traffic."

"I'm terrified and you're making fun of me." He shrank back in his chair. "I don't like how this is going, Vern."

They were sitting in Brent's den, the window bricked over so he'd feel safe, a rug pushed against the crack of the closed door so nothing could crawl in.

Vern sighed. "Sorry. But can't you see how frustrating this is for me? I'm only trying to get you to take another perspective on things, yet have to be so careful how I talk to you. So, how do you know your wife's going to, uh, do what you said?"

"The way she was eating dinner. Oh god, the delicate way she picked at her steak, how clumsy she was with the fork. I knew her instinct was to bend over her plate and suck out the juices. Every once in a while she'd glance up at me. Alert, hungry. She's been weaving a web around me, Vern, and tonight she's going to finish it. The tip of her toe is keeping in touch with it. Waiting for the right moment to pounce."

Vern glanced at the clock. "Even though we're colleagues, I'll have to charge as though you came to my office."

"I know it's late. I'm such a damn pest!"

"Don't call yourself that. It doesn't help your condition any."

"I know. I'm not improving. I'm getting worse."

Vern rubbed the back of his head. "We've been through this, Brent. You're allowing your fear to overcome reality. You've allowed the attitudes of the neurotics you treat to take hold of you."

"But you don't know what it's like! That—that *feeling*. I'm getting it all the time now, like some kind of horrible sixth sense. I walk in a room and just know there's a spider in it somewhere. Up in a corner. Crawling down the triple dresser. They say there's always one within five feet of you, hiding, watching. There's one in my *bed*, and I'm *married* to it!" He shuddered.

Vern filled his cheeks with air and let it out with a pop. "The Araña are an intelligent and well-meaning race, Brent."

"You always say that. But—."

"They've lived among us for a long time now. But they don't *marry* humans. Why would they?"

"To propagate the species," Brent said in a hollow voice. "To turn us into *them*."

"That makes no sense at all. They're perfectly capable of reproducing among themselves."

"Oh? What about climate change? Pesticides. Hormones in the food. Maybe all that's affecting them. Or maybe they just want to get close, to lull our fears, so they can wrap us in silk and suck the life out of us."

Vern leaned forward and looked at him with that half-patient, half-exasperated gaze. "If that was their intent, wouldn't they have done that already? Think things through, man! The Araña knew humans would be repulsed by their looks, so they helped us anonymously for years. They even shared their advanced technology with us."

"Yeah. The World Wide Web. We should've known what they were even then."

"They're not spiders. They are an example of convergent evolution. Life that develops on similar-type planets often have similar forms."

They've invaded our movies with spidermen," Brent insisted, "trying to make us think they're our friends."

"Come on. What about movies like *Tarantula*. 'Crawling Terror 100 Feet High!' Hardly designed to nurture friendship."

"*You* come on. Those movies were trying to tell us the truth, only we didn't listen. Were any of them successful? Star anyone famous? Of course not. The Araña made sure of that."

"All right," Vern countered, "but what about *Arachnophobia*? It's about this spider coming to America to find true love. A heartwarming story, really, and full of humor. I knew the screenwriter. Did you catch the film's resurrection allusion?"

"No."

"It stows away in a coffin, then crawls out. Get it?"

"It crawls out to *mate*. Then thousands of its kids go running amok. You call that a resurrection? Don't you remember the scene where—."

"Listen. This isn't about the movies. It's about your illness, Brent."

"They're out to get us."

"On the contrary. You're a psychiatrist. You should know how sensitive the Araña are. Many of them were terribly affected by the constant waves of repulsion coming from the humans they wished to befriend. You can only face so much of that, you know, until you begin to believe it, believe you are ugly and creepy. Your fear of them is irrational, and you're projecting it onto your wife. You know this. I've certainly explained it often enough."

"But you don't know how it *feels!* Night after night, I stare at that dark hump lying beside me. I edge as far as I can get from those hairy legs."

His neighbor frowned. "You're upset that Amber doesn't shave her legs?"

"No, I'm upset she's a goddamn spider!"

Vern leaned forward intently, almost eagerly. "Are you actually seeing that?"

"Well, no. It's a *feeling*, like I said. A very strong feeling. But I know something about these Araña that no one else does." He glanced around and lowered his voice. "They're shape-shifters."

Vern groaned. "First they're vampires. Then they're spiders. Now they're shape-shifters. They're whatever you need them to be so you can continue in your paranoia."

"So you're blaming me for my own misery."

His friend threw his arms up. "Impossible. This

whole *situation* is impossible." They looked
other a moment. "So what are you going to d(

Brent shifted uncomfortably on his chair. ᵾ~ᵧ
spray? An ax? She's too big to step on, for godsake."

Vern looked alarmed. "No, no! No violence. You
don't want the law involved, do you?"

"What? For killing a spider?"

"For killing your *wife!*"

"But what can I do? I can't stand living like this
anymore."

"I can see that," Vern said thoughtfully. "Well,
there's one thing that sometimes works. Imagine the
worst was true. Imagine—as vividly as you can—that
you are married to an Araña."

"They're spiders! That's what 'araña' *means*, you
idiot."

Vern made patting motions in the air. "Think about
it rationally. The Araña are beautiful life-forms. And
that's not what they call themselves, by the way. Their
eyes are like a crown of sparkling jewels on top of
their heads. Their legs are soft and furry. They are basi-
cally shy and retiring, yet industrious and self-
sufficient. And you know, Brent, where's there's a spider protecting the area, no other dangerous insect will
be around. Maybe—and you should seriously consider
this—that's why Earth has never been invaded by hostile aliens."

"*They're* the hostile aliens!"

"Now, now. You're allowing your phobia to creep
into your mind just like the spiders you fear so much."

Brent ran a hand through his hair. "I can't even go
to bed with her anymore. I spend the night in here." He
indicated a mattress on the floor.

Vern shook his head at it, then regarded him. "Listen.

As your neighbor and your therapist, I'm telling you to sleep with her tonight. If you don't want to see her as an Araña, then imagine, as hard as you can, that she's your faithful wife."

Brent made a strangled sound.

"Take my advice, or live in fear the rest of your life." With a sigh, Vern got to his feet.

He left, exchanged a few words with Amber as she ushered him out, and shortly thereafter Brent followed her to bed. In fear and trembling, he tried to believe the creature lying beside him was his beloved spouse, faithful in spite of his supposed mental illness. He heard the stealthy rustle of the sheet as she rolled over, and all he could imagine in the dark was the avid stare of her jet-black eyes, the lightning-like lunge and grasp.

He woke with a start. Something had bitten him on the neck. With a cold lump of dread in his stomach, he turned, then screamed. *It* was leaning over him, its many eyes looking down at him, its many legs touching him all over. He threw off the covers, stumbled into the bathroom, and flicked on the bright light. He blinked, momentarily blinded—then screamed again. It was in the mirror: a hairy Araña waving claw-like pedipalps.

He whirled, but no one was there. Only himself. Awash with horror, he turned back to the mirror. As if viewed from a telescope, the alien face jumped out at him: bristled, mandibled, and fanged. He looked down at his body: at the ventral plates that covered his lungs, the purple markings on his abdomen, the four legs that held him up, the other four that grasped the sink. He could see behind him with the eyes in back of his head.

The Araña he'd been in bed with scuttled quickly to his side. "It's all right, my honeybee. You're all right." The words sounded strange, made up of clicks and hisses, but he understood them.

"I'm not all right," he choked out. "You bit me! You turned me into this!" His own voice clicked and hissed.

"I bit you, my sweetmeat, but only so you'd see yourself as you really are. It's a kind of shock therapy Vern thought might work. Now just calm down. I've called him."

Instinctively, he backed into a corner and crouched onto the tile floor, trembling. After a moment he realized he could use his two front eyes to see things that were down the hall, then switch to a secondary pair to examine the tiny hairs on his leg. No wonder his face in the mirror jumped out at him like that: he was using the wrong eyes. He mentally examined his body. The backache that had bothered him lately was gone, and so was that twitch in his knee. He *had* no knees. He stretched a bit on all his legs and felt spry and supple—able to scuttle up the wall if he wanted to. He could sense the delicate changes of air pressure rippling over the floor tiles. A nice warm high was coming in from the south.

"You're beautiful, darling," Amber crooned. "So handsome, and in the prime of your life." She busied herself in the opposite corner for a moment, then stepped aside. "Look at this, dear." She'd made a web, just like in that story for kids, with "*I luv you*" written inside it.

The long heart over his abdomen warmed, and it must have shown in his eyes.

Cocking her big spider-head like a puppy, she caressed him with her two forefeet. It felt good. She continued until every hair on his body shivered with pleasure.

Now that he truly looked at her, he saw she was gorgeous—graceful and slim, with delicate, tapering legs. He couldn't help himself. Gently, he reached out and stroked her.

"Welcome back, my darling," she whispered.

Vern jumped in—the real Vern. He radiated happiness and relief. "It was a gamble," he said, grasping Brent with the prehensiles on his forefeet. "We weren't sure what would happen. But you came through! It worked." He rubbed his secondaries together. "This is the first time such a serious case of AAP has been cured among us. I'm going to get the Parker Prize for this."

"AAP?" He seemed to remember hearing something about that years ago, but it didn't really pertain to his patients.

"*Auto-arachnophobia Projectio.* Your specialty was working with the few remaining humans who are afraid of us. Their repulsion and horror got to you, and made you terrified of who you are. So you denied that and decided you were human."

"The truth kept trying to come out," Amber said, "but you projected it onto me as something terrible." She rubbed against him. "All this time I knew you were in there somewhere, my warm little bundle."

Brent rubbed back, relieved to be himself again. "Thanks for sticking by me, my dear."

He touched heads with Vern to offer congratulations, and in doing so caught another glimpse of himself in the mirror. A thrill of pride ran through him. His palps were enlarged, the tarsus at the ends fully mature. He was much better looking than the human he thought he'd been.

All along he was right, though. Crazy, but right. There always was a spider within five feet of him, but it had been himself.

He and Amber went back to bed, and he settled into the embrace of his sexy, multi-legged wife. She began stroking him again, driving him crazy, and so what if she was much bigger than him? That's what made her so dangerously exciting.

ONE LEVEL DOWN

Perhaps Isabel can go one level down, but what will follow her back up?

A soft snick caused Isabel to look up from her chair. By the light of her lone candle, she saw that the door to the basement, always kept closed, had edged open.

It was past midnight and she was alone in the house. Her ex-husband had taken off months ago and her daughter had moved in with her druggie friends. Sitting quietly in the semi-dark was Isabel's way of trying to relax, but now she tensed, staring at the long black crack.

The furnace must have done it, must have caused some kind of draft that pushed the door open. *Just shut it firmly*, she told herself, *and go to bed*.

But how could she fall asleep, wondering if, as soon as she left the room, the door had silently opened again? She'd lie there, thinking about the black crack, imagining a creak in the hallway outside her bedroom door.

"*Confront your fears,*" Dr. Progressi would say, "*you're an adult woman, Isabel. Isn't it time you took responsibility for your life?*"

She pushed off the warm afghan, the one her mother had crocheted for her before she died, and moved toward the basement door. She opened it all the way and looked down. The wooden stairs, painted grey years ago and showing signs of wear, disappeared into the gloom at the bottom. She heard nothing, but it was as if something down there whispered: *I dare you.*

She had to do this. If she didn't, her fears would win. They would rise through the floorboards and take form next to her bed. They would slide into her dreams and, like the hand of frost touching the surface of a pond, shiver them into nightmares. She couldn't do anything about her daughter or her ex, but she could do something about this.

Her hand reached for the light switch, but she didn't flick it on. That would be admitting her fears, masking them, and not dealing with them. This was a confrontation with the dark, and it had to be face to face. Gripping the handrail, she went down. The upstairs warmth bled away; the black opening before her grew larger. A step, and it touched her nose; another, her lips; and with one step more, engulfed her sight.

She swallowed. *I'm not afraid*, she told herself. This is my house, my basement, my choice.

But now she wondered. Why was she really doing this? She sensed the vast, low-ceilinged chamber all around her, felt the utter stillness, and somehow the question seemed irrelevant. For reasons she couldn't explain, *why* had no meaning now; there was only must.

She smelled mold, felt subterranean dampness against her face. The chill of the cement floor seeped through her slippers. All she had to do was make her way to the far end of the basement and come back.

With her arms out like feelers, bent at the elbows

like a snowplow, she took one step at a time. She couldn't see a thing, but this was a known place. She stored things down here, once-useful things that had been part of her life above.

But which are now buried alive.

She caught her breath. Don't think about that. Don't think about the spider that might, even now, be descending on its thread toward my hair. Just move.

She edged forward, reaching for the pool table. Her fingers touched the reassuring practicality of the plastic cover and for a while the edge guided her along. Then it unraveled into obscurity, leaving her fingers reaching out into emptiness.

Panic roiled in her stomach. She breathed, in and out, and the panic subsided. Right above her head was the solid floor of the kitchen and the living room which she'd walked on for years, never thinking of what lay beneath. The phrase—"what lay beneath"—made her uneasy and panic threatened again. But wasn't that only a movie title? She had to keep moving and stop thinking.

But she couldn't see. Not a spark of light. A thought rushed over her like a cold river: What if she'd gone blind?

It could happen in an instant, from a stroke, from an aneurism, from stress. She'd always been afraid of the optometrist more than any other doctor, avoided looking at the poster of the veined eyeball, stiffened when he turned off the light in the tiny room, fought down panic when he aimed the blinding beam into her eye.

Don't go there, she ordered herself. *I'm fine. I won't make myself fail.*

She veered to the left, hands out, until her fingers

touched wood: the door frame of the furnace room. She took a one step through the opening. Faint light from the small, high window revealed the bulk of the old furnace inside. It should've been replaced, but they couldn't afford it.

The furnace was quiet, perhaps sleeping; its multi-armed ducts twisting into the gloom. The small room reminded her uneasily of a story she'd seen on Channel Seven News, of that kidnapped girl who'd been thrust into a padded underground hole and kept there for years. The hole was sound-proof and black as ink. The victim never realized where she was, or that her family lived only a few blocks away.

Stop it! I'm no victim. I've always hated that word. And now I've already made it half-way, to the farthest corner. But she dreaded the way back. That was when things might get bad. The dark let her in, but might not let her out.

No, she chided herself. *Don't allow your imagination to get out of hand. You can do this.*

One step at a time, she moved forward, her arms moving like feelers. Images jumped into her head, amputated snippets of things she'd heard, read, seen on TV. They stitched themselves into shambling terrors that shouldn't exist. Physicists spoke of dark matter, of multiple universes and many dimensions. With only a shrug of its shoulders, reality could shift, could edge her into another time and place. She could be slogging through the sewers of an alien city, or running in mind-less horror through the tunnels beneath an abandoned asylum. Is this what it felt like to be buried alive? To pound your fists on the coffin lid, to scream yourself hoarse, to realize no one will hear you?

Wasn't that how she had lived up above? There

were times she felt like a flat figure spread out on a page, while a mad child scribbled over her mouth and eyes with a fierce, black crayon, leaving her voiceless and blind inside the tight confines of her skin.

Stop it! Why are you doing this to yourself?

Something behind her growled. A throat rumbling with phlegm, gargling bilge. Her heart jumped. Insanity was as close as the darkness against her face.

It was the sump-pump. Only the sump-pump. From above she'd heard it a thousand times. Down here, it was much louder. With a thump, the sound stopped. She heard the silver echo of dripping water, then a soft *sluck*. Like suction-cupped arms unwinding from the hole.

Heart hammering, she thrust the image aside, breathed, forced herself to take slow and deliberate steps forward.

Surely she should be close to the stairs by now; surely she should be discerning at least a glimmer of light from above. But she didn't. Her eyes, wide open and staring, were filled with forms that crawled over the blackness. Her fingers touched the cold roughness of a pole and she clutched it for a moment.

I will not give in to fear, she told herself. *It would flash into mindless terror, pull me into the mind of a cornered rat. Breathe. There is nothing behind me, no thing watching from an invisible corner.*

She took another step, then another. Dim light revealed the stairs. Relief cascaded over her as she reached out and grasped the handrail. Then, so anchored, she turned and looked back, into the cavernous dark. She dared not smile, dared not exhibit any sign of triumph. But she thought: *I did it. I won.*

Do it again, came a sly whisper. *This time let me touch the back of your neck.*

No. She'd done this once and wouldn't have to do it again. Not looking behind her, she climbed the stairs. Firmly, she shut the basement door. It was over.

Except the room she'd been sitting in seemed subtly different. The air stirred in the dimness, as though a wraith has just passed through. The candle-flame strained against its wick. Shadows gesticulated on the walls, urging the flame to break loose of its moorings, to become a were-light floating through the room. The coffee-table crouched on the floor, seeming to breathe as the candle-flame swelled and thinned. Her reflection wavered over the window-panes, like a stranger lurking outside the house.

She extinguished the candle. The TV's blank eye followed her as she walked into the dark of the hall. No sense turning on the lights. The glare would only allow an observer from outside to see she was alone.

As she brushed her teeth, she became aware of her shadowed image facing her in the mirror, and looked away from it. She usually left the door to the bedroom open, but this time closed it. She climbed into bed and hitched the blanket up to her neck. Heart pounding, she lay rigid.

But why? There was no one in the house, no one standing outside her bedroom door. She'd faced her fears and conquered them.

A slow movement drew her eyes to the foot of her bed. Something was coalescing in the squid-ink darkness.

It had followed her up from where it lived—one level down and always there. The blanket began slipping off her. The thing in the basement was determined to reach her. It had nudged one door open and passed through another.

With a whimper of terror, she grabbed the blanket. *Oh, God, clutch it, fight it, scream and rush for the light!*

Or—the thought came—let go. Let the blanket go, and allow it to slide gently into unseen hands.

JAKE AND JAMAL

A journalist, troubled by a story he can't forget, wrestles with the realization that the darkness surrounding it goes deeper than he thought.

I never saw the body, never got photos, never interviewed the grieving relatives. The story came from the principal and the police report, and that was that. Page eight, I think, about five inches. No quotes, no byline. It happened years ago, so why can't I forget it?

Back then I dealt with the facts, or what I would have called the facts. The who, what, when, and where—but not the *why*. It's always the *why* that gets you, isn't it?

They were about thirteen years old. According to the principal, Jamal was big for his age, but slow. He lived with his grandmother in a mobile home park. The other kid, Jake, was an honor student, a popular boy whose parents owned a house in the ritzy part of town. The principal never described either boy, but I just assumed I knew what they looked like. They each fit perfectly, you see, into my stereotypical world.

Jake was supposedly Jamal's only friend. He'd taken Jamal under his wing, so to speak, as if he were an angel. That angel thing bothers me too. What's the saying? "If you see an angel on the road, run the other way?" Maybe Jamal should've done that.

Jamal was accused of killing his only friend after school one day by repeatedly bashing his head against the sidewalk. The principal said that witnesses told conflicting stories about who started the fight, and Jamal couldn't remember.

At first, of course, I assumed it was Jamal. I wondered if Jake had gotten any warning. Did he see a strange look creep over his friend's face and ask what was wrong? Did he fight back? He must have felt crushed by betrayal, horribly surprised at how strong his friend turned out to be.

Jamal must've been blind with fury, or maybe he laughed in exultation at the rare feeling of being in control. When his friend went limp, when he saw the blood pooling, maybe his eyes widened in horror at what he had done. Maybe he went dead inside and stayed that way the rest of his life. I never found out.

Yet here I am, going through life on my last quarter-tank of gas, and I really should be focusing on my final destination. But instead, I'm remembering this. The story is like a black crow in the birdcage of my mind, fluttering against the bars. Why—after all these years of reporting on wars and shootings and natural disasters—should this incident stick in my mind?

Perhaps because, like those other events I mentioned, I painted it in vivid contrasts of dark and light, and placed it within the unyielding frame of good versus evil.

But then, as time passed and I thought about things, I asked myself: how can we tell which is which? Heck, our species ate the fruit of the knowledge of good and evil, and so we ought to know. But eating that fruit was the worst thing that ever happened to us. It brought the delusion of omniscience. So in all the wars ever fought, both sides are positive they're in the right. In every school shooting, we're certain who the victims are. In every earthquake or hurricane or forest-fire we see the diabolical hand.

Except then we find out more. The shooter was mentally ill. The war was started by a lie. Earthquakes are the result of plate tectonics, without which our planet would be as dead as the moon. Hurricanes force people to wonder about their ecological mistakes. And remember that big fire in Yellowstone Park? Lodgepole pinecones were cracking open in the heat and tossing out seeds by the millions, right in the midst of the flames. Can you imagine that? Seeds not just surviving; but proliferating, soaring, *reveling* in what we called a disaster.

So what happened between those two boys? Over the years my mind constructed various scenarios in an effort to make sense of it all.

Perhaps, in spite of his popularity, way down deep Jake wanted to die. He instigated the fight, knowing he would lose. Perhaps he lived with a black hole eating away inside him, with an emptiness that swallowed every drop of joy he had ever scraped together. Perhaps he lived in a home of upper-class addiction, of meaningless getting and spending that was strangling his soul and leaving him a zombie. Better to have the life pounded out of you than to live like this.

Or the black hole may have been inside Jamal's head. He'd see it everywhere, day after day, like those floaters you get in your eye. Maybe he'd been shouted at, hit, rejected. Maybe he suffered terribly from psychological wounds that had been ignored. Maybe he cried out for help—like we always discover after the fact—and no one answered.

The other kids could have goaded Jamal into it, promised they'd be his buddies forever if he beat up his best friend. They could have told him all kinds of lies, or even truths: "Hey, Jamal. Jake's just pretending to be your friend. Behind your back he imitates your stutter, makes fun of your clothes." Jamal could have been the victim of a cruel manipulation, the victim of an even greater dark.

Or the whole relationship may have been sinister. Jake saw his friend as a kind of pet, or pet project. He demanded hero worship, demanded constant gratitude for the saintly sacrifice he was making by tolerating the other kid's presence. Jamal would have resented this role—the role of the well-treated slave, the homeless man who must prove himself worthy of the coin tossed to him—until he couldn't stand it anymore.

Maybe Jamal watched his friend hanging out with other boys and a terrible fear rose up inside him. His friend Jake was getting tired of him, would leave him, would become one of *them*. Maybe Jake *was* getting tired of him. Who wants to be saddled with someone who clings, but would never fit in?

Some people at the time said Jamal was just mean, rotten to the core, an incurable sociopath better not born. They hoped he'd get tried as an adult and die by lethal injection. A lot of hate there, a lot of darkness, surrounding someone who was really just a kid.

Was it hate or righteous judgment? Was Jamal the hapless scapegoat every tribe seems to need? Do I see him most nights on Action News? Is he the bank robber, the rapist, the boyfriend who shakes the baby?

Now that I think about it, he seems to be everywhere, wherever we need someone to blame.

And what about Jake? Is he the smiling mask that hides an ugly face? Maybe I see him on TV, too. The preacher who touts family values but has a mistress on the side. The congressman who rails against child porn but has a computer filled with it. When I see that, I can't help feeling that the hypocrite—the one who wears the mask—is the biggest sinner.

I've been thinking all this for years, but only recently have I noticed something strange. Apart from each other, Jake and Jamal aren't quite real. If we endow one with a halo and the other with horns, if we make them black and white cut-outs that exist in only one dimension, how can either be human? And, perhaps most frightening of all, how can we be?

Ah, Jake and Jamal. Why can't I forget you?

ADVENT

Experiencing a crisis of faith, Miles seeks out three figures around a bonfire. But there's a fourth, whom the firelight doesn't reach.

Miles found them sitting on a grassy hill, watching a bonfire twist orange spark-trails into the night sky. All four turned their heads toward him as he approached.

An old man with a wooden staff across his lap studied him. His eyes were deeply circled, like the knots in a panel of knotty pine. "You've come a long way, haven't you," he said.

It was only from the crowded city below, only from an unremarkable life, but it had taken him ten years. He bore the weight of a vast and growing loneliness, made even more painful because it was wrong to feel it. To acknowledge that hole within him was somehow betraying all he had been given. A wife, a son, a house, and a paycheck—-all that should be enough for any man. But it wasn't. The familiar sense of loss, which he tried to keep at bay, filled his throat. He nodded, unable to speak. Yes, he'd come a long way.

The second figure, a woman wearing a plain white gown, indicated that he should join them. A crown of acorns and laurel circled her long hair. "Ah," she said "you need to find meaning in your life."

The kindness in her voice touched Miles, and he swallowed the lump in his throat. "Sorry," he managed to get out, "but I already know there isn't any."

"Is that why you tried to end it?" the third figure asked. Between the flames, Miles saw a muscular black man wearing a goat-skin. His brown eyes glittered.

Miles lifted one shoulder in a shrug. "We're born alone," he said, "and die alone. Then there's nothing. What kind of an answer can you give to that?"

The old man pursed his lips and nodded. "What do you mean by 'answer'?" he asked. "Do you mean 'answer' as in 'What is the answer to one plus one?'"

"Or," continued the woman, "do you mean 'Here I am, knocking at the door; please somebody answer?'"

Miles thought about the compost pile at the edge of their yard. Every year it was the same. Throw the grinning jack-o-lantern there, where its face eventually caved in and got spotted with mold. In time, dead poinsettias joined it, to be covered by snow. Then came the wilted Easter flowers. They disappeared under the grass clippings that he dumped over them after mowing the lawn. "If," Miles said, "if there was someone on the other side, then I would want them to answer that door. I would be desperate for them to answer. But there's no one."

"If you're so sure of that," the old man asked, "why are you here?"

"He wants a story," the goat-man said with a sneer, "but only one about himself."

"Every story is about ourselves," the old man said. He looked at Miles. "Just make sure you don't end it before it's really over." He gestured for him to sit down. "We tell only one story here. It's about ancestral grace."

Miles had never heard that phrase, but sat.

"Once upon a time," began the woman. She stopped, then said in a different tone: "Quite a phrase, that. As if we must thumb through the dimensions to find our place. Or flip through the book of evolution to find where we began. But anyway. Once upon a dream-time, we were primitive furry mammals clinging to each other in our burrow. It was as if we all shared a common skin, but we were still lonely." A faint smile of reminiscence touched her lips. "But even then, with barely a brain between us, we strained to hear a word we didn't know."

"I remember," said the goat-man. "Dinosaur footsteps thudded above us, and bits of soil filtered onto our heads." As if to brush them out, he swept a hand over his nappy hair and grinned at Miles. "We'd be there still, but hunger called us out. The first thing we saw was this." He gestured at the sky and a huge yellow moon sprang into view, so big it startled Miles. The goat-man laughed. "Scared you, eh? It was a lot closer then than it is now."

"But it was the stars that fascinated us," said the woman. She waved the moon away, to reveal a myriad of stars strewn across the deep night. They shone rusty red, hot blue-white, even a faint green. "Fire-flies filled our stomachs," she said, "but, ah, how the stars filled our eyes!" Rapt, her head back, she gazed at them for a while. Then with a flick of her fingers, the glory disappeared.

"At night we slept in trees," she continued, "where branches cradled us and warm breezes rocked us, yet we dreamed such restless dreams." Her dawn-grey eyes turned to Miles. "The rich earth called us by day, sending delicious scents that floated in the air. They were

60

like seeds blowing in the wind, and we had to stand on two legs to see where they went."

The old man rapped his staff on the ground. "What we're saying, boy, is that we were born with an empty place inside us. You aren't the only one; it's part of who we are. So as we grew, that empty place grew too."

Yes, the empty place, Miles thought. *The place where you wanted to paint every red door black.*

"But then a strange thing occurred," the woman said. She formed a circle with her hands. "It was as if the world in which we floated began to stir, to whirl faster and faster around the empty place. Our little womb-world became too small to hold us, until"—her hands flew apart—"it pushed us out. All of a sudden we were separate. An angel had cleaved us with a flaming sword. We looked into faces that weren't ours, and would never be ours again."

The goat-man shrugged. "Our ape-mothers cared for us but never understood us. How could they? We were something new. We were humans, and our instincts were blossoming into wisdom." He peered at Miles through the flames. "Did you know the word for 'wisdom' in the bible is *'sofia'?*"

"I had an Aunt Sophie once," Miles said. "She had six kids, then died."

The goat-man gave him a pitying look. "So succinct, the way you describe a life. How shall I describe yours?"

Miles looked away. "That was a cheap shot. I never knew my aunt and lost track of all my cousins."

"So if you're done investing your life with yet another tragedy, I will continue." The goat-man raised his eyebrows and waited. Miles said nothing, and he went on. "*Our* 'Aunt Sophie' was a new spirit inside us.

She showed us how to fashion arrow-heads, follow the herds, spark fire out of rocks." He pointed into the distance and craggy forms appeared. Holding wooden spears and torches, they trotted single file on a plain. They were oblivious to the wispy female figure, slight compared to their bulky bodies, skipping around and through them. With a snap of the goat-man's fingers, the vision fled.

The old man leaned over and tapped Miles' knee. "We're telling you," he explained, "that we were always like you are now, on a pilgrimage. We trudged into the desert silence and listened for a word. Like the prophet Isaiah, we gazed at the clouds, hoping the word would rain down." He fluttered his fingers in illustration. "We studied the soil, hoping it would bud forth." He made of show of peering at the ground.

"If you're living in the desert," Miles said, "you're not hoping for anything. That's what living in the desert *means*: you are incapable of hope."

The old man nodded. "But even in the wasteland, there are seeds." His hand was suddenly full of them, and he poured them from palm to palm in a golden stream. "They fascinated us. We noticed that where seeds fell, green things grew." He threw the seeds into the air. They glittered for moment among the bonfire's sparks, then unfurled into stalks and leafy curlicues that filled the space above their heads. "There was a word for this process, you understand, but no one knew what it was."

"Then came a day," the woman said, "when I discovered my mate lying on the ground, so still that flies crawled on him." Her eyes grew distant, and the sky-plants fell in a shower of red and gold leaves. "He didn't wake up, no matter how hard I shook him." She touched her abdomen. "Pain bloomed inside me, but I remembered the seeds. I dug a hole in the ground and planted his body there."

"Ah," said the old man with a gentle smile, "our first farmer." He glanced at Miles. "See? We were already making connections between death and resurrection."

"How can there be a connection," Miles said, "between a reality on one end and a myth on the other?"

The old man frowned. "Well, I don't know. To me they're both the same. The great myths always express a deeper reality. That's what true spirituality is all about."

Miles shoved his hands into his jacket pockets and sighed. "I haven't been to church in years. I wish I *could* go there. I wish I *could* find meaning in a plastic rosary or a ceramic Jesus."

The woman snorted. "Don't worry about church; it's mostly patriarchy and dogma. I knew nothing about it back then. All I knew was that my mate was alive in my dreams, or spoke to me in my thoughts, but most of the time he wasn't around. More and more of us experienced that. It was a mystery, and it ground into us like a fire-stick into wood."

"We painted the dead bodies with blood-red clay," the goat-man said, "but they didn't come alive. We beat drums, but their hearts didn't take up the rhythm. We tried to explore the aching hole inside us by crawling into caves. We wanted to penetrate the mystery, to grasp the unknown"—he raised his hand and clenched it into a fist—"and make it ours."

"We failed," the woman said, "but we left behind the prints of our open, empty hands."

Miles took his hands out of his pockets and looked

at them. They had caressed his wife, held his child. In the bonfire's light they jumped now into shadow and now into light. They'd picked up the handgun in the dresser drawer.

The old man sighed. "And so time passed. We produced all sorts of things that caught, for a moment, our attention." Without looking up, he waved his hand negligently above his head, and cartoon drawings appeared in the night sky. Yachts, designer jeans, spiked heels and giant TVs floated by, and Miles watched them parade into oblivion.

"Hordes of us," the old man continued, "ebbed and flowed over the land, leaving the flotsam of our languages behind. Our prophets sat on their mountain-tops or under their trees, and they heard whispers, as if from fragile shells that spoke of the sea, but none of these whispers were the word."

"We don't need more words," Miles said. There were too many already, swirling in a chaos of advertising, emails and social media.

"But none," said the goat-man, raising a finger," fill the ache inside." He glanced at the fourth figure, who had been silent all this time and who still said nothing. The firelight didn't reach where he sat in shadow.

"Going into caves didn't work," the goat-man went on, "so we explored the big wide world. We left our footprints in strange places, even on the moon. We played dangerous games and summoned the red-mouthed god of war." He raised his hands and visions sprung into being above his head: sword-wielders clashing, a battlefield wreathed in cannon-smoke, mortar shells pumping out shock and awe. He snapped his fingers and they sank into the earth.

The old man leaned toward Miles. "Throughout all

our history we'd fed stories to each other, around campfires, or on silver screens. Some of the stories promised a word, but most were transmitted into the air and got lost in space."

Lines of sorrow appeared on the woman's face. "We looked up in the dark, in the shadow of all we had made, and we cried: *'Why, oh God, amidst the billions of suns, are we still so alone?'*"

The fourth figure, still in shadow, stirred slightly. Miles sensed an intensity there, a kind of compassion, straining forward.

"Ah," the woman continued, "but out of this galaxy of iterated need, a light shines out on a winter night." She looked up, at a lone candle set in a window in a stone wall. "Compared to the thousands of stars that looked down from far off, it was nothing. But we knew it burned for something essential."

"We had moved out of Africa," the old man said, "up the steppes, over the great seas; but always the light of our longing looked out of that window." The night breeze lifted strands of his grey hair as he watched the candle-flame gutter and leap.

The goat-man leaned toward Miles. "Our brains didn't know what we wanted; our tongues couldn't say. But our hearts knew. We desired Emanuel with a fierce desire. We longed for the God-with-us who would always stay."

"Simply put," the old man said "we wanted a god who would keep us company."

Something his dad once said jumped into Miles' mind. He'd gotten home late from a party and Dad was sitting on the front porch, smoking. Miles joined him and neither said anything. Dad just stared at the sky. He was a teacher, and Miles asked him if he had a hard day at the high school. Dad said something, so low Miles barely heard, that scared the hell out of him. "The eternal silence of these infinite spaces terrifies me." It was the first time Miles saw his father as a terribly vulnerable human being. Shortly after that Dad went the same way Miles tried to go, but made a better job of it. Dad could've used a god that kept him company.

The woman turned to look at Miles. "For so long," she said, "we lived with a wisp, a wraith, an inconceivable dream. Oh God, we would swallow our fear before any angel, if only she announced the word."

In the night's quiet the bonfire burned. In Miles' throat, something strained and burned.

"A star of such intensity," the old man said, "cannot endure. It can only collapse into a black hole, into a well that drags in the debris of our long search. Splinters of hope, shards of doubt, the cutting edges of it-never-can-be—it all swirls in and scrapes at the barrier, at whatever blocks the giving and receiving that makes whole the heart."

The old man looked through the bonfire and addressed the fourth figure, who was now standing. "Just like us, you endured that passion. You were always pulling at us: the singular attraction that turns everything inside out."

Moving into the light, the fourth figure resolved into a young man, his eyes shining. "I saw your flame because it was my own." His voice vibrated with emotion. "We ached with the same desire; with a longing that reaches, grinds, and painfully pushes; until on a night in Advent—"

"—at last the barrier breaks—" the goat-man cried,

"—and full of grace," the woman exclaimed, "love pours through!"

Irresistibly drawn, Miles rose to his feet as the others spoke in chorus. "Bone of our bone, seed of our seeds, you are the Word spoken at last."

"As you enfolded me," the young man said, "I enfold you." He opened his arms. "I am the hunger that made humans seek life, the stars that made them leap, the seeds that had to die. Mine are the eons and the seasons juggled for your delight. Mine is the singularity inside your very core."

Miles stumbled into his embrace. He leaned into it and its strength surrounded him. Warmth poured in, rose, and filled him to the brim. It leaked out of his eyes and down his cheeks. It was joy always sought, largess barely hidden: love beneath, beyond and within.

From the very beginning, they were never alone. From the very start, they were graced.

The waves of emotion gradually lapped smaller and smaller, then settled into a deep, wide calm. He opened his eyes, filled his lungs with cold clean air. The figures and the fire had gone, but the hilltop wasn't empty. Miles joined the half-seen forms of those who'd come up before him, and walked down the hill toward home.

END OF STORY

Donald and Alice get more than they bargain for from the writing class they're taking at night. This story won an honorable mention from a Writer's Digest Popular Fiction Contest and was a finalist for a Penumbra Magazine themed issue.

Mrs. Pyara hummed a Tamil folk song as she sorted index cards for her cookbook. The one for Mixed Vegetable Kootu she put aside. It would be perfect for her next big family festival: Arudara Darshanam. It was the time when Lord Shiva danced as a red flame under the full winter moon, his divine body glowing like the miraculous Hanukkah lamp and making God's newborn baby smile from his bed in the hay. So many festivals of light during the darkest months.

She smiled, then sighed. It was her busiest time of year; and now she had to join that adult ed class. Two of the more unpleasant participants would certainly need her recipes if they were to celebrate the upcoming time of grace.

Donald Dukavich hated his name. Kids in school used to taunt him: "Donald Duck! Donald Duck!" Especially Billie Glish's gang, who liked to get him alone in the boys' bathroom. So he'd thought long and hard about his pen name and chose one that sounded cool: Donnie Drummond. He was fifty-two, over-weight, and had never been cool.

A self-addressed envelope lay unopened on his desk, and he could feel it staring maliciously up at him as he clicked into his e-book account. In spite of his holiday mark-downs, there had been no book orders last month. Or this month either.

He picked up the envelope and tore it open. "Dear author," blah blah blah. "Darkweb Press" stamped at the bottom. Above it a large, confident hand pro-claimed: "Too violent, lacks passion. Sorry, T."

Anger churned in his gut. Who the hell was T? Toni, who barely passed American Literature in high school? He hated women who usurped men's names, but who didn't have the balls to admit that violence *was* passion. He tore the letter into pieces.

He was getting upset. Bills were piling up. He hadn't taught an adult ed class in a while, and now might be the time. Donald pawed through a pile of papers until he found the township newsletter.

It was cold in the dining room and Alice pulled her sweater closer. She picked up the township newsletter and pushed away her tomato soup. It didn't taste right—too thick and it needed salt. Her gaze fell upon an article. A writing class was offered in the evening, when she could get away. But dare she go? Alice pic-tured herself shrinking under the bright classroom lights, surrounded by inquisitive strangers, everyone looking at her.

Yet she had to get out, had to get a life. The idea both terrified and excited her. She read the notice again.

*

Fiction Writing for Pleasure and Profit took place at the community college on Thursdays from seven until nine pm. Donald got there early and, after stomping snow off his boots, walked down the deserted hallways, looking for an isolated rectangle of light. But no lone teacher was working late. Of course not. He'd learned a long time ago that teachers were never around when you needed one.

At class-time, he found his students consisted of geezers and foreigners, including a dusky woman from India apparently, who held a plaid plastic bag stuffed with papers on her lap. Behind her sat a wispy nonentity, almost invisible against the beige walls. According to the attendance sheet, her name was Alice Marlow.

The students were supposed to read something they'd written to the class. He listened to Alice drone on, her story filled with lots of bad dialog from people supposedly in group therapy. She stopped reading and looked up. Sandy hair, eager brown eyes. If she had a tail, she'd be wagging it.

"So what do you think, Mr. Dukavich?" she asked.

It was garbage. "It lacks passion, Alice." She cringed in her seat, which gave him that satisfying squirt of power he hadn't felt in a long time. "Your main character has no character. Why should we care about him?" He addressed the class. "That's your assignment for next week. Write a character sketch that makes us care."

"I am writing a cookbook," Mrs. Pyara said in a clipped Indian accent. She looked around at the students with a smile. "It shows my people care. We believe good cooking is a service to humanity."

"You're in the wrong class," Donald said. "This is for fiction writers."

"No, no," she protested. "I am most surely at the right place. At registration the lady said as long as I pay, cookbook is fine."

"I'm sure she did." He grinned at the class, then turned back to her. "So make your main character a salami." Everyone tittered, but the woman didn't seem to understand why. Donald shook his head. Damnfool immigrants. They refused to blend in, but always wanted special treatment.

His dinner that night was leftover Chinese. He ate it cold, sitting with his bare feet propped up on his recliner, then leaned back. The moon was shining in his eyes. With a curse, Donald got out of his chair and jerked the drapes shut. It was time for Sex House 8 on TV. He watched the show in the dark, but it wasn't enough. His hand shook as he took off his glasses and put them on the end table. The writhing images were reflected in the lenses, and he thought of Alice—eager, tail-wagging Alice.

Chewing her thumbnail, Alice sat at the dining room table and stared at her notebook. Maybe the writing class was a bad idea. Her teacher's eyes looked so big through those thick glasses, and he stared at her too much. An odd stare, hungry yet wary, like that of a fat diner afraid that the dripping-red piece of meat on his plate might jump up and smack him in the face.

Maybe she should have volunteered at a nursing home. But the thought of those dry, emaciated bodies, those saggy necks, made her stomach turn.

She left her chair to look out the window, where an icy moon was rising above the bare trees. She'd have to wait until early spring to see the Full Worm Moon, as the Farmer's Almanac called it. It was the time when worms in the damp earth rose in response to the ghostly lunar beckoning. She imagined them writhing in an ecstatic, veiny mass.

With a sigh, she made her way through the dark hallway to the kitchen and searched the pantry for a can of meatless spaghetti with sauce. Every day it got harder to keep her vegetarian vow.

Donald raised his eyebrows. Alice had fallen silent and she peered at him from over her paper. "So," he said, "this Jerry is your compelling character. What's so compelling about him?"

Alice flushed. "He's tortured."

"What makes him tortured?" Alice shrunk into her seat. Maybe he could make her disappear altogether. "How old is he, Alice? Is he married? Why is he in group therapy?"

With each question he stepped closer, until he was standing over her. She turned pale, which was gratifying. She ought to be afraid of him, the little runt.

Alice flicked on the light in her dining room and averted her eyes from the mirror above the antique credenza. "Look in the mirror too often," her mother always said, "and the devil will appear." The thought of her face morphing into something that leered and thirsted made her heart pound. Alice sat down at the high-backed chair and opened her notebook.

There was something wrong with Mr. Dukavich. A shiver ran down her arms when she thought of his moist, fleshy neck, the vein throbbing in his temple when he looked at her. He shouldn't bully her so much, demand so much. It wasn't fair, when she was trying so hard. Biting her lip, she looked into the middle distance, then picked up her pen.

Donald called on Alice to read. She hunched her shoulders and cleared her throat. When she was finished she looked at him, biting her lower lip.

He almost laughed in her face. Every sentence was a disaster. But then he caught her strange expression. Was it speculation? Cunning? She had described her hero, Jerry, as a heavy-set man with dark eyes—a mirror-image of himself. She had written that Jerry wanted to do terrible things.

She knew something. She suspected. And she wanted to play games.

Excitement rippled through him, but he managed a cool smile. "What terrible things does Jerry want to do? Tell the class, Alice, exactly what you imagine he's up to."

Alice felt her face get hot. She shouldn't even be thinking about what her character did, much less talk about it in front of the class. "I—I'm not sure. Something bad."

He shifted his position and his glasses momentarily turned opaque, as if eyes with no pupils stared down at her. "Describe it."

His voice was low and silky, and she knew for sure now: something was wrong with Mr. Dukavich. "People shouldn't write about bad things."

"Oh come now, Alice. We're all adults here. This is an adult ed class, remember? You said your character wants to do terrible things. So what are they?"

He was enjoying this, she realized. "I can't think of anything."

"We're wait-ing," he said in a sing-song voice.

"She cannot think of anything!" Mrs. Pyara frowned at him. "Leave the poor child alone."

Donald shot a dirty look at her and went back to Alice, who felt her face flame. "Next week you're going to get up here in front of this class and tell us what Jerry's secret is. You're going to reach into your gut, Alice. You're going to pull out something red and alive and splatter your pages with it."

The next day, Alice called him at home. "I can't write about violence," she said in a small voice. "Or sex either."

His heart jumped, then started to pound. "I see," he said carefully. "Listen, Alice. Let your imagination loose, and don't judge your character. Just describe what he does, what he thinks, how he feels."

"But he's perverted!"

"He's not!" He had spoken too loudly and lowered his voice. "You said he was tortured."

There was a long silence. "I'll try, Mr. Dukavich."

Alice hung up the phone. She was upset and had to eat. Taking a place at her dining room table, she felt something heavy in her sweater pocket. A tube of lipstick. How did it get there? She must throw it away; scarlet color didn't belong on her lips. And she shouldn't see Mr. Dukavich again. It was disgusting. Dangerous.

Alice picked up her plate and slurped down the tepid red juice left from her steak. Mr. Dukavich was making her write about things she shouldn't. Someone should make him pay. Someone should give him what he wanted. "The worst thing you could ever get," her mother used to say, "was exactly what you wanted."

*

Donald arrived at class the following week irritated at the slow-moving traffic. Hadn't these people seen snow before? His mood improved when he found that Alice had made changes in her story. Jerry Javelin was now Damon Devereux—his same initials. She dropped a few tentative hints about the darkness in Damon's soul, his irresistible compulsions.

Donald pushed for more details, but she acted coy. He pushed further, and that excited her. He could tell: she wanted to be driven.

After class she asked him not to make her read in front of the students anymore.

"You think I'm too hard on you? I'm not. You're on to something with this Damon character."

"But he's creepy. He's cold and unfeeling, but underneath there's a—a fire." Her eyes glowed as she looked at him. "Maybe he's just toying with his therapy group. Maybe he's trying to find someone vulnerable."

"So he's a serial killer, looking for his next victim?"

She laughed nervously and dropped her eyes. "I could never write about that."

"Do it. I dare you. Bring me more next week and I'll critique it at home. But make it something worth my time."

Biting that lip, she turned and went out.

When he left the building, the weather had cleared up but the parking lot was covered with two inches of snow. Mrs. Pyara stood outside the door, probably waiting for her ride.

"A beautiful evening, is it not?" she said. "Especially for Arudara Darshanam."

"Aruda what?" he asked, pulling out his car keys.

"It is our holiday. It is a time when God draws closer to us." She looked into the sky and smiled. "See the beautiful moon he has placed in heaven?"

"I don't answer rhetorical questions," he muttered. He clicked his car remote and out in the dark two red tail-lights sprang into life. They were like the eyes of a predatory beast, and for an instant he panicked. But that was ridiculous: he had everything under control. The foreign woman had disappeared by the time he scraped off his windshield and drove away.

He read Alice's chapter in front of the blank TV. It was full of sexual tension. Just as he had suspected, she was tantalizing him, teasing him. Bland little Alice knew exactly what she was doing.

She didn't show up at the next class. Donald found her phone number on the registration card and called her at home. "You're such a coward, Alice. Where's your next chapter? I thought we made a deal."

"I don't think I should come back, Mr. Dukavich."

"Listen, Alice. Next week is our last class. I don't want to see talent like yours going to waste."

"Yes, but—."

"Tell you what. I'll end the class early and we'll meet at Starbuck's. We'll go over your next chapter together. Your dark side is emerging, Alice, and you shouldn't let anyone stop it."

Coffees steaming in front of them, they sat at a table in an out-of-the-way corner to discuss her latest chapter.

"Damon can't, like, help himself," Alice said. "Killing is what keeps him alive." Her eyes met his.

"He's so wounded, yet so dangerous. No one under-stands him."

"Except you."

She looked down, carefully folding her empty sugar packet in half. "He's hiding something."

Donald leaned closer. "But you know what it is, don't you Alice. Tell me."

"What if he's like—like a vampire or something?"

A thrill surged through him. "So. Your hero is a powerful and sexy hunter of the night."

"It was just a thought," she said hastily. "I should-n't—."

"You should. You should definitely go with this idea. Violence is passion, Alice. Remember that."

A half-smile worked its way across her face. "A vampire!" she breathed. "But I could never—."

"Oh yes you can. Get into his skin. Feel with his gut. That's how you control him." As if she could ever control anything.

"His girlfriend still loves him," Alice mused. "Briana suspects what he is, but she still loves him."

Donald's heart pounded; the old tension was rising up. "You're getting to the climax, Alice. Your story is working up to an orgy of blood and murder."

The words hung in silence, and for a moment he thought he had gone too far. "Think how that would add to the drama. Briana knows what he is, knows that *he* knows she knows, but just can't help herself. They need each other, don't you see? In order to get what they want."

"Well," she said, "sort of. But what if my neighbors ever read—?"

"To hell with them! You're more than a pallid Alice." She'd played the game with him so far, teasing and tantalizing, and he wouldn't let it end yet. He had his own ending in mind.

Alice looked down. He found he was clutching her wrist, and let go. "You've come a long way, Alice. Come just a little further."

She pushed her empty coffee cup away. "I already did." She took a folded sheaf of paper from her purse and thrust it at him. "Just—just read it at home." Alice grabbed her coat and rushed out.

Sitting in his recliner, Donald read a chapter that made his pulse race. Briana and Damon played their deadly duel, and it left him sweaty and wanting more. Just like Alice planned. He phoned her and, smug little fool that she was, she came.

The minute he locked his door behind her, she knew the game was over. She fought him, knocked off his glasses, scratched his face; but it was only foreplay. He flung her onto the sofa and choked her screams into silence.

After a while, satiated at last, he leaned back. Her eyes were open, staring blankly. End of story, pathetic Alice. End of story.

But it wasn't. Alice sat bolt upright, grinning horribly. With superhuman strength she flipped him onto the floor and straddled him. Her burning eyes fixed on his neck and came closer.

When she was finished, Alice leaned back, wiped her mouth, and spoke to the still body beneath her. "You prodded and goaded and dug up what you wanted, dumpy Mr. Dukavich. Not quite the story you had in mind, was it? But a satisfying end for me. It's been a *very* long time."

There was a knock at the door, and Mrs. Pyara swept in.

"Omigod!" Alice exclaimed, jumping to her feet. It was the Indian lady from class. But she looked different. She seemed taller and terribly intimidating. For an instant, red lights danced around her head. Alice blinked and the illusion disappeared.

Mrs. Pyara's eyes traveled from the man on the floor to Alice's face. "Hmm," she said. "You are both quite unpleasant people at the moment."

"It was his fault!" Alice cried. "He wanted it. You saw what he did to me in class."

Donald sat up, clapping his hand to his neck. "*She* wanted it! A man can only take so much."

Mrs. Pyara shook her head. "You have done unto others what you would not like done unto yourselves."

"He's a murderer!" Alice exclaimed. "He's killed I don't know how many people and tried to kill me too."

"She's a bloody vampire," Donald said. "She was stalking me."

"I was trying to keep it all buried—"

"—but she kept digging it up."

"Yes, yes," Mrs. Pyara said, "even from the beginning: blame, blame, blame. 'The woman you put here gave me to eat.' 'The snake made me do it.' The fact is both of you ended your story too soon, before I had a chance at it."

"I'll tell my story the way I want," Donald said.

"I love the way you ended up in it." Alice sneered.

"No wonder you're both so hungry," Mrs. Pyara said. "Your souls are too thin, and your hearts are starving."

Donald looked down and shuffled his feet. "Why should you care?" he muttered.

"It is who I am," Mrs. Pyara said.

Alice's eyes grew moist. "It's too late for either of us, Mrs. Pyara."

"Nonsense. Collaborating with me on my cookbook will be just the thing." She sat down at the kitchen table, waving at the fast-food wrappers and porno magazines, which abruptly disappeared. She opened her large plastic bag, and the smell of cardamom and ginger, jasmine and nutmeg wafted out.

"I have recipes here," she said, "for tangy curries and sweet pudding with raisins and cashews. My specialty is chicken tikka—so succulent and juicy! And none of that canned tomato soup dumped on."

"I didn't have any dinner," Donald said to Alice. "You weren't all that satisfying."

"I didn't have dinner either. You're all fat, Mr. Dukavich, and no substance."

Mrs. Pyara eyed them with a tempting, conspiratorial look. "But for Arudara, I have my Adai cakes that never crack, and Vegetable Kootu with yellow moong dal. Come. Taste and see."

Food was now frying on the stove or baking in tandoori pots, and the mouth-watering smells drew them both to the table. Donald and Alice sat and eyed each other warily. Mrs. Pyara whisked open the drapes and the light of the full moon rushed in.

By its light, Donald peered around the room. "My apartment seems, uh, bigger now," he said. "It's glowing with—candles? And who are all these people? Their faces are blurred."

Alice stirred uneasily. "I don't see any people," she said, "but I hear music and laughing."

"It's just my family," Mrs. Pyara said, "come to eat with us." She patted Alice's hand. "You cannot see them very well yet, but give it time. Meanwhile, let us begin."

It took a while, but they learned how to eat properly, prepare good food, and serve it to others. In the fullness of time, their souls got bigger, their hearts expanded, and they joined a much larger family whose story, they eventually discovered, had no real end.

Author's note: A plaque hangs in my writing room, which recounts an old Irish saying: "Everything will be all right in the end. If it's not all right, it's not the end."

Questions for Discussion

1. Which is your favorite story in Night Cruiser? Why?

2. Psychologist Carl Jung defines the shadow as "everything the subject refuses to acknowledge about himself." These can be inferior character traits, unmet challenges, or our own dark side. Of the ten stories, which ones would you say shine a spiritual or insightful light on how the different characters deal with their shadow?

3. Which story did you find most creepy? How might it relate to your own fears?

4. Julian of Norwich, a 14th century mystic, famously wrote that "All shall be well, and all shall be well, and all manner of things shall be well." Which story seems best to echo her belief?

5. Individuals must deal with their shadow, but so must larger communities. Which story do you think focuses on a shadow that haunts today's society the most?

6. In "Persons of Marred Appearance," what is the shadow that Deirdre faces? That Deacon William faces? How is Chris a wounded healer?

7. The stories in Night Cruiser, the author said in an interview, are really more about hope than horror. What do you think?

8. Taking all the stories into consideration, how many examples can you point to in which something bad got redeemed? Are there any instances in which a character refuses redemption?

Thank you for taking the time to read Night Cruiser. If you enjoyed it, please let your friends know that and consider posting a short review on Amazon and/or Goodreads. Word-of-mouth referrals are an author's best friend and much appreciated!

I invite you to sign up for my private email list for giveaways, sneak peeks, and notices about my other books. I won't spam you or share your address with anyone, and you can unsubscribe at any time.
Sign up here: www.veronicadale.com

About the Author

Veronica Dale writes genre-bridging fiction that includes fantasy, romance, psychological intrigue, and spirituality. Her stories have received commendations from *Writer's Digest, Writers of the Future, Readers' Favorite Book Review, Midwest Book Review,* and the National League of American Pen Women. Much of her work has roots in the psychological concept of the Shadow and in Tolkien's belief that even the worst catastrophe can be redeemed. With a background in pastoral ministry, Vernie is a member of Phi Beta Kappa, a graduate of the Viable Paradise Science Fiction and Fantasy workshop, a Goodreads Author, and an established author with Detroit Working Writers. Visit her on at her website at www.veronicadale.com.

Also by Veronica Dale

Blood Seed:
the riveting mix of dark fantasy and romance
that launches the
Coin of Rulve series

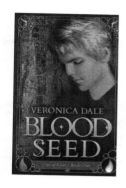

Sheft: maligned, hunted, chosen
Mariat: the woman determined to save him

Sheft grows up stalked by an ancient evil that lives in the nearby Riftwood. He learns how to evade it, but the effort comes at a cost. Certain there is something dangerously wrong inside him, and already despised as a foreigner, he must keep himself apart. Yet, beyond what he had ever dared to dream, Mariat breaks through his isolation, and the two fall in love. But when Sheft is forced to take part in the secret Rites of the Dark Circle, he confronts the true horror arrayed against them both. He must decide between protecting the one he loves, or embarking alone on the dark journey his destiny demands.

"A new approach to this genre"..."a beautifully crafted page-turner rendered with stunning depth"...
"intense, powerful and compelling."

Look for *Dark Twin:* Book Two of the powerful new fantasy series *Coin of Rulve*

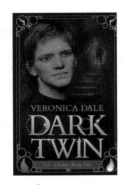

Teller: damaged, driven, destined
Liasit: dares to confront him with his true name

Snatched as an innocent boy into the Spider-king's subterranean stronghold, Teller has no idea he is the emjadi, one of twin brothers called to walk the redeemer's path. Mind-probes twist his memories of home and he grows up as the dark rebel, simmering with hatred for the extended family he thinks abandoned him and the lord's acolytes who are ordered to corrupt him. A mysterious parchment hints of a chosen one with a name similar to his—and a connection to the twin brother he barely remembers. But when he discovers within himself the legendary power of fire, Teller must decide if he's the savior the beautiful slave Liasit needs him to be, or the lord's enforcer in a reign of bondage and addiction.

About the
Coin of Rulve
Series

Coin is a series for adults or mature young adults that incorporates themes from epic fantasy, romance, and myth. Its four-volume story arc tells how Sheft and Teller, twin brothers who are challenged to accept their own power for good, travel a dark road toward a distant light. They find tender love, face bitter heartbreak, and undergo trials that can kill them, while through it all feel a compelling call they don't understand. Yet they are also mystics who experience not only a divine presence, but also the dark night of the soul. As many of our favorite tales do, *Coin* has at its core a moral premise that is inseparable from the human psyche. For Sheft and Teller, the spiritual quest feels more like a forced march, but they also discover how tragedy can lead to providential grace.

"An original tale with a strong story/character arc for the series as a whole"… "keeps getting better and better"… "a page-turner" … "wonderfully sympathetic characters and gifted prose"…"Wowza!"

www.veronicadale.com

Made in the USA
San Bernardino, CA
02 March 2016